Alan
Gibbons

hold on

Dolphin Paperbacks

In memory of John Sorrel
1989 – 2005

First published in Great Britain in 2005
as a Dolphin paperback
by Orion Children's Books
a division of the Orion Publishing Group Ltd
Orion House
5 Upper St Martin's Lane
London WC2H 9EA

1 3 5 7 9 10 8 6 4 2

Printed in Great Britain by Clays Ltd, St Ives plc

ISBN 1 84255 176 0

www.orionbooks.co.uk

Alan Gibbons

Alan Gibbons is a full-time writer and and lecture, the major book festivals. He lives in Liverpool with his wife and four children.

Alan Gibbons has twice been shortlisted for the Carnegie Medal, with *The Edge* and *Shadow of the Minotaur*, which also won the Blue Peter Book Award in the 'Book I Couldn't Put Down' category.

part one

The Citadel

Annie

Wednesday, 3rd September

I know what I have to do. Now I'm home I mean to get justice for John. I just need to work out how to do it, how to make his killers pay. It may come as something of a surprise, but this is no whodunit, I know exactly who's to blame for his death. I know their names. I know where to find them. All in all, I know everything about them. It isn't as if they're hiding. They're out there. They're waiting. Everything is in place, the drama, the cast of characters. All that's needed is a hero or, God help me, a heroine.

I've known John's killers for years. We inhabit the same small world and that world starts here, at the school gates. I wait for them, squinting against the whipping September wind, struggling to control the sledgehammer beat of my heart. The school is Grovemount High, a monstrous hybrid of two existing comps, Grove Street and Mount Carmel. Get it? Grove-Mount, Grovemount. Whoever came up with that little gem is either bound for a knighthood or a one-way ticket to the funny farm. Together the two sites have been reincarnated as a kind of breeze-block squid that reaches its grey tentacles into the town centre. Though the buildings aren't pretty, it isn't a bad school. I've always got along OK, until now.

This is where the killers will have to pass me, at a windy junction between the second and third tentacle. Very soon, for the first time since it happened, I will see them. Nothing has been done about it. It's incredible, but not a single one of them has been brought to book for killing a sixteen-year-old boy. None of them have paid for what they did to him, and it was calculated, yes, mean, spiteful and utterly deliberate. They can carry on walking around, having fun, getting on with their lives. You'd think it had never happened, which is why it hurts.

John was my friend.

Here they come now. I thought I was ready for them but I didn't expect this. Not for a moment did I dream they would be quite so cocky, so dazzlingly, maddeningly *unconcerned* by what they've done. I always imagined there would be something shame-faced about them. Their guilt would have grown, tumour-like, eclipsing everything else. Really, that's how I pictured them, those four boys walking past me hunched and ill-at-ease, darting shifty looks in my direction. It seems I was living in a dream world.

I mean, look at them. They're smiling, laughing. As they approach, they're swaggering, in a line, across the road. Their blazers are billowing in the breeze. It's one of those iconic images. I'll remember this as long as I live. They could be in an advertisement. No, better still, they could be starring in a video on MTV, the clean-cut boy band. But they've got a secret, haven't they? They're cold-blooded killers. See that? See how the sun picks out their features, falling on their cheekbones, illuminating the planes of their faces. It highlights their eyes. In the movies the bad guys are often ugly, twis-ted inside, twisted outside. Their faces betray their poisonous hearts. But these boys, they are so alive, so wholesome-looking, so . . . cute. Oh, shut up brain, why do you have to make thoughts like that come to me?

These boys remind me of a TV drama I saw once, about a group of lads preparing to go to war, sure that the precarious future belonged to them. That's how they look, but for them the war is over. They weren't the brave, embattled few. No, they were the dark legions and their Blitzkrieg has left my friend John broken, derelict. When the onslaught got too fierce his defences crumbled. In the end, he gave in. He was the casualty.

I hate to admit it, but last year I would have given anything for one of them, especially Matthew, to ask me out. I so wanted to hang around with them. Maybe they weren't the brightest blades in the drawer, but they were definitely the coolest. All the boys wanted to be them, all the girls wanted to be with them. But the thought of any of them, even Matthew, touching me now, well, it makes my skin crawl. I'm twelve months older but I feel as though I'm half a lifetime wiser, all because of what happened to John.

There they are, pleased with themselves, revelling in the sheer joy of being alive. John isn't. He will never feel the sun on his face the way they do. He will never walk through the school gates the way they are walking now. And it is down to them.

He's gone, my quiet friend. This summer John took his life. Yes, when it all became too much he swallowed a bottle of pills, the contents of several different bottles they say. I try to imagine him looking at the label, opening the cap. Somehow, I can't visualise the moment at all. But he did it, he sank a lethal cocktail of drugs and then he lay down to die. By the time his parents found him he was stone cold, not a human being any more, a body, a corpse, a thing.

A hailstorm of questions rush towards me. What was he thinking about as he took them? Did he really mean it? Was it that calculated? Was there really a moment when he chose to go to sleep and never wake up? That's what I find so hard. I can't stand the thought of him sitting alone, staring at the bottle of pills, believing there was nothing in the world left to keep him going. Why didn't he trust anyone enough to reach out? Why didn't he ask for help? I find the world blurring in front of me and I start inventing excuses in case anybody notices me crying. It's the autumn sun, something in my eye. Who am I kidding? I should tell them exactly why I'm crying. It's what they did, what the school allowed them to do.

It all comes down to one question. How do I do it? How do I take hold of John's hand from beyond the grave? How do I get justice for him? I feel physically sick at the very thought of what I have to do. I can actually feel my breath shuddering through me, scouring the linings of my confidence. I'm not brave. I never have been. Who is at my age? All I ever wanted was to be ordinary, one of the crowd.

So many thoughts rush through my mind. Will I be able to

find the words I need to confront them? Will I ever dare? Oh, this is just great. I'm all questions and no answers. But there is no other way. It's up to me, Annie Chapman. I'm the one who has to do this. I'm the one who has to get them to feel shame, to at least own up to what they did. Isn't that what justice is, the causing of remorse, the burning of the features of the dead into the minds of the living?

You can't bring back the dead. But you can get people to acknowledge them. You can give them recognition, a life beyond life. I suppose that's what I want, something like the bleached stone pillar in the town centre commemorating the war dead. I want a monument to John, to his suffering. But who am I to even think of taking it on? I'm a typical sixteen-year-old girl. All these years I've gone with the flow, then suddenly there is this huge responsibility thrust upon me. Even my own mum and dad would like me to keep quiet about the whole business. It's all best forgotten. Get on with your life.

'Don't go storming in, Annie love,' Mum warned when I told her what I planned to do.

Storm in? I've never stormed in my life. I do what most kids do: I get by. Who do Mum and Dad think I am, Lara Croft? Still, parents don't always think straight about their kids, though Dad for one was thinking straight. He put it bluntly: 'Annie, I forbid you from raking this up.'

There you go, Dad on his high horse. He *forbids*. Then it was Mum again, all sweet reason: 'Nothing is ever as simple as we think, Annie. Those boys have been interviewed. If the police can't do anything, then what makes you think you can?'

I spent most of last year trying to get these very boys, these thoughtless killers, to notice me. I would even bump into them between lessons, accidentally on purpose. I swear they didn't even turn their heads. What John needs is a heroine but the world is all out of them. Most of us are satisfied to be the chorus, singing the same tune, shrinking back into the same shadows. All the people I ever looked up to, all the people I would have trusted to keep John safe, all the people who should be helping me now, failed him. So it's down to me. I'm the one.

The tallest of them, that's Matthew Rice, looks like butter wouldn't melt in his mouth, doesn't he? What with the blond hair and the good looks, he's got half the girls in school sighing over him. To think, not that long ago I was one of them.

The boy alongside him is Luke Woodford. He's the leader. You can tell by the body language. The others defer to him. He pulls the strings, comes up with the one-liners, sets them off laughing. Seems he's got an acid tongue on the quiet. John told me. No, that's not right. My friend didn't tell me in so many words. I read it in his diary. That's where it was all written down, how they hurt him, how they killed him.

The other two, Anthony Fraser and Michael Okey, they're nothing special. They're hangers-on, that's all, the kind of flotsam and jetsam that bobs aimlessly on the school tide, just glad that they are the merchants of bile, not its victims. They did nothing to help John. They joined in humiliating him. They laughed at everything Matthew and Luke said. I bet they even egged them on. They might not be the ringleaders but they did their bit. They're guilty too. If they'd once confronted Luke and told him to leave it, if they'd once got him to see that John had had enough, then maybe he would have survived. Maybe the citadel would have stood.

I'm still standing by the gates watching them, wondering how I can ever bring them down, when Bryony puts in an appearance. Bryony Calder, my best friend.

'Hi you,' she says, kind of shy. She's got uncertainty written in her face. She isn't sure what to make of the Annie Chapman standing in front of her in her brand new navy blue uniform.

It's the first time I've seen Bryony in almost a year, you see. I flew in from Canada a few days ago. Twelve months we've been out there. What with the jet lag and the unpacking, I haven't had time . . . No, that's an excuse. I could have found time. Friends do that. They find time but there doesn't seem enough space in my life for anyone else. John is taking all of me. The fact of his death seems to blot out everything else.

I've chatted to Bryony on the phone, of course, lots of times. We talked when I was over in Departure Bay. We texted. We e-mailed. But since this thing with John, I'm finding it hard. Deep inside, I know that nothing is going to get back to normal until I do something about it. Since he died, I don't know how to do all the fun, trivial things. It's as though there's a barbed hook caught in my heart and the line keeps tugging it. Every time I so much as think about smiling, doing my hair differently, laugh out loud at something on TV, there it goes. Tug. I know whose hand is pulling it too. It's John. It's his hand on the other end of the line, telling me to bring the truth to light.

'Hi you,' I say, my voice dying away as I hover round Bryony.

That's the way we always spoke before I went to Canada, sort of *Friends*-ish. We didn't treat anything very seriously then. Why would we? The only real dramas we encountered were in the books we read, the movies we watched. It was all crisis by proxy. There were no shadows over our lives. Well, the usual ones: boys, growing up, living with yourself when you look in the mirror. We used to joke about the *Friends* thing. I was Monica, dark-haired, a bit obsessive and uptight, but nothing too heavy. She was Rachel, blond, prettier, more filled out than me, more shapely, a bit ditsy too. Is that a word, ditsy? They used it in *Friends* so it must be. Anyway, Bryony is definitely ditsy.

'Who're you looking at?' she says, turning her head. 'Matthew? Setting your sights a bit high, aren't you?'

I feel the tug. There's the hint of a sting in my chest, as if a tiny fibre is being drawn through my flesh. It must be real, this thing called heartbreak. If this is what I feel because Bryony has mentioned one of John's tormentors, then the real thing, heartbreak itself, must tear you in two.

'I'm not looking at Matthew,' I tell her, blushing hotly, allowing my irritation to show. 'I'm just . . . looking. I've got to point my eyes somewhere, haven't I?'

Irritation is what I call it, shame even. I feel the familiar itching between the shoulder blades. I'm ashamed that I didn't go right across and slap him. I hate myself for not screaming at the whole lot of them, accusing them of murder. John's avenging angel, that's what I should be, a Fury taking them each to their own personal Hell. So easy to say, so hard to do when my every instinct is to get back into the routine, to fit in.

'OK,' Bryony says, enough of a smile in her eyes and on her lips to tell me she doesn't believe a word of it. I don't blame her. Last year I probably was looking at Matthew that way. Me and Bryony, we used to give the boys marks out of ten and Matthew was a definite nine. The marks were just for looks, you understand, we didn't get near them, not ever. No, we yearned from afar. They went chasing after the Year 12 girls. We didn't think we had a chance. Knowing what I know now, thank goodness we didn't.

Imagine . . . Oh, just imagine if we had got together. If Matthew and me had been an item, Michael and me, any of them, just think what I would be feeling now. Would I have looked at John the same way? Would I have signed up for this mission? Might I even have joined the ranks of his tormentors, or at least gone along with the teasing? It doesn't bear thinking about.

'Going to registration?' Bryony asks. 'Or are you going to stand here all day? What's your registration group, by the way?'

'11KL,' I tell her.

She gives a high-pitched squeal. 'No way,' she gushes. 'That's mine too.'

'I think it's intentional,' I say, distinctly underwhelmed at the prospect of being in the same registration group. 'You know, ease me back into things by putting me in the same group as my best friend.'

'So we're still best friends?' she says.

I look at her. She's got her head tilted to one side, blond hair spilling into her eyes the way it always does, just the flicker of doubt in her blue eyes.

'Yes,' I tell her, 'still best friends. Honestly, Bron, did you really think I'd change?'

The blue eyes leap. That's when I notice. I've lost sight of the four boys. The four boys? That doesn't sound right. I don't know what I ought to call them, but boys isn't it. Boys don't do what they did to John. Pack hounds do that.

'What about Miss Leather, then, ' Bryony says. 'A bit of a turn-up for the books, wasn't it?'

'I think she prefers to be called *Ms* Leather,' I say. Ms Leather – not Miss, you understand – is one of those women who is still making a statement about herself. While some people seem to have given up on feminism and think that a Page Three girl can be a role model for women and lap-dancing is in some weird way empowering, Ms Kathy Leather has always stood firm. All this lipstick empowerment, it's the same old sexist crap in new clothes. Ms Leather's my role model. I think I must have had some sort of crush on her when I was younger. Of the half-dozen women teachers on the staff she's the only one who can really handle the boys, even Luke Woodford.

One time he made a joke about her name, loud enough for her to hear. The boys started calling her Miss Whiplash. Get it, leather, whiplash? Boys' humour, if anything is. She started out ignoring it, then they said something that went way past the mark. Ms Leather tore into them for that, not in a hysterical way like some of the other female teachers would have done. She didn't go shrill at all. I admired her for that. There was an inner calm about her, but there was steel there, too. She met Luke's studied glare of defiance and faced him down. No, she made Luke and his crew look about six inches tall. My heroine, Ms Leather. But that's all in the past. Even she let John down in the end. She must have. She was there all the time and she stood back and let it happen. Because nobody came to his aid. Nobody called off the hounds.

'She doesn't prefer Ms anything any more,' Bryony says. 'Ms Leather is a Mrs.'

Bryony didn't tell me this on the phone, or maybe she did but my mind was too full of John to take it in.

'So how come her class is still called 11KL?'

'Because she married Mr Linklater, that's how come.'

Mr Linklater! This guy is to men what the bulldog is to canine-kind.

'No!'

'Ye-es,' Bryony says. 'I'm sure I told you.'

'Maybe,' I say. 'Anyway, tell me more. Come on, give with the gossip.'

'Are you sure you want to know?' she says, acting all coy.

Well, I just leap on her. 'Don't forget I can tickle the truth out of you,' I say.

Bryony dissolves into a fit of giggles and I join in. For the first time, I'm back. I'm the best friend Bryony remembers. Her eyes light up and I'm glad. I hate the luke-warm person I've become, scared of smiling, ashamed of being in a world that John has left. But I've got him tugging on the line and he isn't going to let go.

'Oh yes,' says Bryony, her words accelerating as they gush out of her. 'I knew about it way before anybody else. I saw them in town, holding hands.'

'But Linklater,' I say, 'the Missing Link, how could she?'

Bryony shakes her head demonstratively. 'I saw them snogging. It wasn't a pretty sight.'

'Snogging!'

Bryony grins. 'Well, more a peck on the cheek really.'

'Talk about Beauty and the Beast,' I say.

'Quite.'

By now we are passing the library. I glance inside. Mrs Kruger is hanging up her coat. She's the school librarian, another one who let John down. That's where he used to hide, the library. It was his sanctuary. But the boys got in there, too. She let them.

'Got something on your mind?' Bryony asks, obviously noticing the seriousness creep back into my face.

'No,' I say in my bad liar voice. Why do people do that? When somebody rumbles you, why do you deny it? It's a knee-jerk reaction, I suppose.

Question: Did you eat the last Rolo?

Answer: No. Well, yes, actually.

'Well, yes, actually,' I say, correcting myself.

'Oh?'

'It's John, John Sorrel.'

Bryony's 'Oh' bongs its way down a deep pit inside her. Her face clouds over. The look in her eyes is almost accusing, as if I have mentioned something unsavoury, something best left unsaid. I wish I could start tickling her again and forget John, but the genie's out of the bottle.

'I wondered how long it would be before you brought him up,' Bryony says.

Of course. We talked about it on the phone. She knows I met him in America.

'School's been really weird since it happened,' Bryony says. 'People don't mention it much, but you know it's there, at the back of their minds.'

Good. I'm glad it's there. What right do any of them have to forget him? The teachers, Mrs Leather – I mean Linklater – especially; Mrs Kruger, all the kids, yes, even you, Bryony, you all let it happen, even if it was only a sin of omission. Everybody's guilty.

'There was talk of putting up a plaque,' Bryony says.

This is news to me. 'I got the impression they just wanted to sweep it under the carpet,' I say. My gran sent a newspaper clipping. The head teacher, Mr Storey, set the tone by going on about how there was no bullying problem in his school. You got the feeling everybody was running for cover.

'You could be right,' Bryony says. 'There is no plaque, is there? It never happened. It was a rumour, I suppose. Anyway, it makes sense. You don't commemorate a suicide, do you? I mean, if somebody gets run over or drowns saving a dog, maybe you give them a plaque, yes, maybe then. Not if you kill yourself.'

I stare at Bryony. It sounds as if she's thought about this, especially the bit about the drowning dog. Bryony likes dogs. Save a drowning mutt and you'll be right up there in her pantheon of heroes.

'So why's suicide different?' I say, cheeks burning.

Bryony blinks. I almost yelled that at her.

'Sorry,' I say. 'I didn't meant to sound . . . '

'Forget it,' Bryony says. 'It *is* different though, isn't it? I mean, how can you do that to yourself? He was only sixteen, our age. He had everything to live for.'

How many times have I heard that since it happened? Mrs Sorrel says it all the time. He had *everything* to live for. You know what, that's crap. In John's eyes, he had nothing to live for.

'Are you sure about that?' I say.

Bryony's forehead crumples into a frown. 'What are you saying?'

We've reached our form room. I can see Mrs Linklater at her desk, messing with the stupid palm pilot they use to register us. What next, electronic tagging, nano-technological implants? I can just see it, *Terminator 4: Registration*.

'I'm saying . . . '

Somebody bumps into me. I look round and see Matthew Rice. I stare for a moment. I don't believe it. What's he doing in my registration group? Some irony, huh? The killer is in my registration group. You know what he does then? He smiles at me! A thought flashes through my mind. Once, twelve months ago, it was me bumping into him, accidentally on purpose. Could he be . . . ? I catch Bryony's eye and she's smiling too. She thinks there's a spark there, between me and this . . . creature. How could she?

'You don't understand,' I say. 'Nobody does.'

'Understand what?' Bryony asks, still looking after Matthew.

'They killed him,' I hiss, staring at Matthew as he takes his seat. 'Matthew Rice, Luke Woodford, they all did.'

from John's diary
Monday, 14th April

Something good happened today. It was a chance meeting. All my life the only luck I ever got was bad and suddenly there's this mad, brilliant coincidence. Of all the theme parks in all the world she had to walk into mine. What are the odds against meeting somebody from school thousands of miles from home? This must be it, that one big, I mean really big – massive actually – really totally massive coincidence they say you get once in a lifetime. What are the chances of that someone being Annie?

We were in the queue for Space Mountain, Mum, Dad, Katie and me. Katie was talking nineteen to the dozen, as usual. She was so excited. She kept saying: 'I don't believe it. I'm in Florida. I'm at Disney.' She'd already been photographed with Mickey Mouse and Goofy, well, some guys dressed up as Mickey Mouse and Goofy. They actually give autographs. Would you credit it? There will be some guy called Richard P. Lawnmower Junior, or Duke McPuke or something, wriggling out of his air-conditioned Mickey Mouse costume in the changing rooms and he's just signed himself *Mickey* ten thousand times. Weird. I wonder if he could be prosecuted for impersonating a rodent.

She's every parent's dream, our Katie. She hugs Mum and Dad for giving her treats, tells them she loves them at least twice a day. She gets just excited enough to tell them they're great parents, but not so much she turns into a brat. I wish I could be like that. But how do you tell somebody you love them when you never know if you'll get it back in return? Me and my parents, we live on opposite sides of a street called trust. It wasn't always like that, not with me and Mum.

I was trying not to show my nerves. About the ride, I mean, not

Annie. I got a different sort of feeling when I saw her, a leap in my heart. You know, it's not as if we were close at school. I hardly paid her any attention at all. She was another blue-blazered girl, another bobbing pony-tail. As for Annie, I bet she didn't know I even existed. I try to look unconcerned about Space Mountain. Dad hates it when I bottle out. He's the original Stress Hound. Everything has to be on his terms, and it all has to go right. I'm his biggest problem. His son the wimp, the apology for a human being. I was making the effort though. That's when Katie gave this huge squeal.

'It's Lauren,' she yelled. 'Look, it's Lauren Chapman.'

Next thing you know everybody's introducing themselves and commenting on what a coincidence it is, meeting all this way from home. Katie and Lauren were in different classes but they knew each other quite well. The only ones who said nothing were Annie and me. She's quite shy, too. We hung back, kind of interested, kind of wary, a satellite circling an invisible planet, until our parents shoved us forward the way parents do.

'You two must know each other too,' Mrs Chapman said. 'You were both at Grovemount High at the same time.'

'Yes,' Annie said. 'Same year actually.'

This is a turn-up for the books. Annie remembers me. She's aware I exist.

'Same year!' Katie squealed, clinging to Lauren as if she would vanish like a mirage. 'Just like us. Oh, this is too fantastic.'

The Sorrels and the Chapmans, a study in symmetry. But before any of us could say another word we'd got to the front of the queue. Annie must have noticed the way I was gripping the safety restraints.

'It's OK,' she said. 'This is the second time I've been on it. There's really nothing to it.'

I think that helped. Anyway, I got through Space Mountain. Not that there's much choice when you're being thrown about at five zillion miles an hour. The stars shone brightly even if it was in a synthetic cosmos.

There was another bonus. With the Chapmans about, Stress Hound was on his best behaviour, unlike the first day of the holiday.

Mum was navigating. Somewhere between Sanford airport and US Highway 192 we took a wrong turn. So Stress Hound's beating the steering wheel with his fist. He's like that. One little thing goes wrong and he flies into a rage. He was just the same when he couldn't manage the automatic gearbox. You could hear his voice echoing all round the Alamo car park. Fifteen stone of testosterone-fuelled spoiled brat is what he is.

'For Christ's sake, woman,' he bawled at Mum. 'Can't you read a map? Haven't I got enough to do, driving, without having to do your job on top? Can't you see I've got to concentrate? All you've got to do is look out for the right turning.'

'I'm trying,' Mum whined, the way she always does.

If Dad's the Stress Hound then she's his Agony Kitten. Honestly, they were made for each other, interlocking pieces in a jigsaw of misery.

'Oh, you're trying all right,' Stress Hound said. 'I wish our Jessica was here. You could always rely on her.'

Our Jessica, my older sister. She did the map-reading last time we came but that was when she was in Year Twelve. I was ten years old and Katie wasn't anything. Now Jessica's doing teacher training in Coventry. She doesn't know how lucky she is to be away from all this. Then again, maybe she does. She doesn't come home more than once a term.

'Well,' Stress Hound barked. 'Come on, where do I turn?'

I think he likes it. Not being lost, you understand – he hates that. No, what he enjoys is beating her up about it, using her as his verbal punch bag. He likes anger for its own sake.

'Well?' he says again.

'I don't know,' Agony Kitten says. 'Isn't there anywhere we can pull over?'

'And how do you propose I do that?' Stress Hound yells. 'Where do I pull up? I know, I'll just slew the car across the highway and get in everybody's way. How's that for an idea?'

His head snaps round at something on the side of the road.

'What's that sign? Bee Line Expressway. Did you get that, we're on the Bee Line Expressway. Well, come on woman, find it. I need to know which way to go next. Now!'

16

Then Agony Kitten's fiddling with the map like a neurotic doing origami and getting in his way so he starts slapping the map with the back of his hand. I want to slap him back but I don't have the guts. I hate myself for not having the guts. Katie winces.

'Are we lost?' she asks.

OK, so where've you been for the last five minutes, Pipsqueak? I keep shtum. Stress Hound goes easy on Katie, same as he always does, same as he did on Jessica when she was living at home. If I'd said it he'd be biting my head off by now. Me punch ball, him fist. Stress Hound doesn't answer. He just screws up his face and blows, like he's got the world weighing on his shoulders.

'We're looking for . . . John Young Parkway,' Agony Kitten says. 'Yes, that's it, John Young Parkway. That'll take us to US Highway 192.'

'So how do we get to John Young Parkway?' Stress Hound asks.

Agony Kitten doesn't answer. Two reasons. For one, she never was any good at map-reading. Plus something just snapped inside her. She's got her lips pursed tight together. Panic has congealed into stubborn resistance.

'Could I see the map?' I ask.

Stress Hound snorts. 'Oh, that's really going to help,' he sneers.

I hate it, the way he does that. Anyway, I take the map and I work out a route.

'I think you can get back down something called Orange Blossom Trail,' I say. 'It'll be either south or west.'

'You think!' Stress Hound says. 'Oh, that's wonderful, that is. You think.'

He's about to try to come up with something witty. You know: *Orange Blossom Trail? He'll want us to follow the Yellow Brick Road next!* Well, that's his idea of witty. Then Agony Kitten sees the sign and he shuts his fat mouth.

'There it is,' she says. 'Orange Blossom Trail. Well done, John.'

Stress Hound doesn't say well done. He doesn't like the way I cut him off in mid put-down. He doesn't say anything. I toss the map across the seat in disgust. For God's sake, Dad, is it so hard to say something nice to me? But he just gets on with the driving. I watch Florida flash by. Stuff the miserable get.

17

It isn't often I could have hugged our Katie – normally, I'd rather cuddle a Mexican Hissing Cockroach – but today I could. The Chapmans were about to drift off when she said it: 'Can Lauren come round with us?'

Lauren obviously liked the idea so, before you know it, we were all hanging out together. I'm not sure the Chapmans were that keen. You could tell by the shifty glances they exchanged from time to time. I don't blame them. Who wants to be stuck with the family from Dysfunctionville, UK? Anyway, they went along with it. We even went for something to eat together. Somehow, Annie and me ended up on a table all to ourselves.

'Where've you been?' I asked Annie, in the same way people in corny old movies ask: *Where've you been all my life?*

That didn't sound right, almost as if I'd been pining for her, which I hadn't. We'd hardly talked at school. No, scrub that. We'd *never* talked at school. We weren't even in the same form, just the same year. Sure, I'd eyed her a couple of times, but then I'd eyed quite a few girls. Lardy boys do a lot of that. Bryony, her friend, was the one I really fancied. She was curvier, sexier, but beggars can't be choosers. It's not like I had my pick of females. I wish! Nobody wants the fat boy. The number of times I've tried to diet. I've even had a go at jogging, but only after dark of course. I didn't want anybody seeing me.

'Didn't you know? We've been living in Canada for the last nine months or so,' Annie said, cutting in on my thoughts.

I knew she'd moved school, but I didn't know she'd gone all the way to Canada. It's a long way to go to get away from Grovemount.

'Canada,' I said. 'How come?'

So she explained, all about Mr Chapman being made redundant and wanting to use his redundancy to make something of himself. They'd organised a twelve month house exchange and moved to a place called Departure Bay. Great name. She says there's a song about it by Diana Krall. Diana who? I prefer Nirvana, the Clash, Coldplay, Snow Patrol. Katie says it's old man's music. I tell her it's better than the bubblegum rubbish she listens to. She says it's miserable. I ask her what's wrong with miserable. She gives me the kind of look men in suits give tramps.

Anyway, I did the maths. If they came out in August they'd got five months left. Mr Chapman has joined his brother's IT company out there. I asked if they planned to sell up and stay for good. By then I had more than a hint of hope in my voice that she'd say no. Please say you're coming home when the twelve months are up. I couldn't remember the last time I'd talked to a girl this long. Maybe if she came home to England . . . I mean, you never know, do you? It can happen to me, can't it? Isn't there somebody for everybody, even the lardy boys? I've seen them in town, big, fat, out of condition guys with the most gorgeous woman you've ever seen hanging on their arm.

'I'm not sure really,' Annie said. 'The year's up in August. Mum and Dad have got to make their minds up by then. I know Mum would like to go home.'

Yes, way to go, Mrs Chapman. My skin prickled. Could this be Fate?

'She misses her parents and her sisters.'

I couldn't help myself. I had to ask. 'And your dad?'

Annie shrugged. 'Dunno,' she said. 'You know what dads are like.'

I do, but not the way Annie meant.

There was one more question. What about Annie? What did she want?

'Me?' she said. 'Oh, I'd like to go home. Departure Bay's a lovely place and all, and everyone is very nice, but it's not home. At Grovemount there was a whole gang of us who used to hang out. I'm kind of on the outside of things.'

It looked like, cut off from that posse of hers, she hadn't found it easy to make new friends. Join the club! I've got friends – OK, there's Peter – but the moment the wolves start circling he makes himself scarce. I can't blame him. Annie changed the subject after that and started telling me about the author of *Anne of Green Gables* who was from Canada and how she was big in Japan. I have no idea why she thought I'd find that interesting – probably the first bit of psychobabble to pop into her head. I think it made her uncomfortable, bringing up how lonely she felt. That's something I recognise, of course, the solitude she's feeling now. That's where I live, in a crystal cell where the walls are lined with loneliness. Sometimes I can hear the echoes of my own screams.

I don't believe it, two good things in one day. I've just heard Mum and Katie talking in the kitchen. Yes, you read me right, I did say Mum. She's only Agony Kitten when she's with the old man. When she's on her own, she's a different person, she's my mum. I wish she could be herself more often. Thing is, I really need somebody right now. Sometimes she's that someone, then along comes Stress Hound telling her to stop mollycoddling me. Mollycoddling! That's his word for any sort of affection. Anyway, we're going to meet up with the Chapmans again tomorrow to go to MGM. There must have been an exchange of phone numbers. There will be no dark echoes tonight, no screams.

Annie

Thursday, 4th September

I don't know if I should have told Bryony. Blurting it out like that, maybe it wasn't the best way to pick up the threads of our friendship after my year out. It's put a distance between us. We didn't exchange a word during registration. Or after. I think it made her uncomfortable. I'd forced her to look into the pit. She lowered her eyes and she barely looked at me again the whole day. I suppose I was including her in it, tarring her with the same brush as all the others. They're all to blame, everybody who let it happen, everybody who ignored John, everybody who turned a blind eye while the pack hounds ripped at him.

Everything seems so cock-eyed. The last time I saw him he was smiling. He was happy. No doubts, no qualifications, no ifs and buts, he was 100% pure-and-simple happy. It was the night before they flew back to England. We all went for a meal together, a Chinese buffet. We cracked open fortune cookies, the way they do in Hollywood movies, and laughed about how much we'd eaten.

'It's a wonder I don't burst,' I said.

'You've nothing to worry about,' John said. 'You're so slim.'

Which was a nice way of saying there's more fat on a matchstick. There was envy in his voice. He wasn't exactly fat and he compared well with a lot of the American kids who are like hamburgers on legs. Over there, you're talking Lard City. He wasn't lean either, though, not like Matthew Rice, and he was painfully self-conscious about it. John carried what my mum calls puppy fat. Which sums him up really, he was like a big, bouncy pup always trying to please me. So there you go, lean wasn't in John's vocabulary. He might crave that cut, sporty look, but it

21

was never going to happen. I felt sorry for him. More than sorry, I felt angry, not at John, but at the goons who teased him. So what if he wasn't sporty-looking. There are more important things. He wasn't bad-looking, in that boy-next-door kind of way, even if he could do with losing the odd pound. The point is, I never heard him say a cruel thing about another human being and that's got to count for something.

'You're lovely,' he said, his eyes steady on mine.

There was a moment's silence, when we exchanged glances, when we remembered an evening a few days before. My gaze flickered towards Mum and Dad but they were out of earshot.

'I won't be for long,' I said, my voice neutral, letting the moment pass. 'Who's going to love me when I'm fat and grey?'

John wanted to say *me* but I didn't let him. That would be just too corny – a creep-out factor of at least eight and a half. Plus I didn't want the pressure of having to say something back. In the end he came out with the oddest thing:

'In my eyes you'll never grow old.'

Typical of John. He wasn't like a teenager at all. He wrote poetry and a diary and enjoyed his own company. Peter's the only friend he ever mentioned. I remember Peter, a quiet boy with wild, unkempt hair, a bit eccentric but pleasant enough. Neither John nor Peter were the kind to hang around the streets, so most evenings I suppose John stayed in, occupying himself. With parents like his, it's a good job he was self-sufficient. Sometimes, it was as if they were so tied up in their own problems – and, did they have problems! – they forgot all about him. He told me once he dreamed of having a window seat. He would be like one of those romantic heroes from fiction, keeping his secret letters and diaries hidden inside it. He planned to write the Great British Novel.

That Easter holiday he was really getting into Dan Brown. He was reading *The Da Vinci Code* and *Angels and Demons*, conspiracy thrillers full of codes and puzzles. That's what had John hooked, the riddles.

I probably blushed when he said it, the thing about me never growing old. I could definitely feel my ears burning. I told him not to be so daft. That was the last time I saw him. He said I was lovely, the first boy who ever did, and I told him not to be daft. Then we all walked out into the car park and the evening heat. John jumped into the back of the Space Cruiser. He waved to me. His eyes were sparkling. Like I said, he was happy, unconditionally, unreservedly happy.

Then he went back. To his death.

The door goes. It's Dad. He's got a job at the PC Superstore in the retail park. He spends his day removing viruses from people's computers. Out of the three of us he's the one who really needed Canada to work. When he got made redundant last year all the air went out of him. He withered like an old balloon after Christmas. Not that Dad ever moans to us. He's not like that. He goes inside himself.

Sometimes he takes himself down to the canal and sits there for hours fishing. If there is one hobby in the whole world I don't get, it's fishing. He took me once when I was a little girl. I was so bored. And all those dragonflies and midges! They hung round me in clouds. They took one look at my fair skin and said: dinner! By the time I got back home I looked like a sheet of bubble wrap. What's more, at the end of the whole sorry shebang you chuck the fish back! Still, it's Dad's thing so who am I to knock it? He isn't hurting anyone. Well, there is the little matter of the odd perch – definite Grievous Bodily Harm there – but that doesn't really count, does it? I can see Dad sitting there staring into the grey waters, trying to make out the shape of his future in the ripples. I wonder what reflections he sees.

'How was work?' I ask.

'Fine,' he answers, then, as if realising he isn't trying hard enough to be Mr Happy Dad, he adds: 'No, good. They're a nice crowd at work.'

I know they're not. I go over and put my arms round him. He likes that. He strokes my pony-tail. Just for a moment he rests his cheek on my forehead.

'Thanks,' he says. 'I really needed a hug.'

Then the moment's over. Lauren comes running downstairs,

a blur of velour track-suit, and flies into his arms. He swings her round, Dad's little girl. On the second turn, he winks at me. Dad's big little girl.

It's Mum next. She walks in wearing her ward sister's uniform. A real study in blue, that's Mum on the way to work. In her flat shoes she looks a lot smaller than usual. Anyway, the shortage in stature is more than made up for by the way she wears her hair. It's drawn back in a tight bun – too tight maybe. It gives her a really bossy look. She wraps her coat round herself. It's warm outside and the coat looks a bit over the top but the hospital doesn't like the nurses going into work in uniform. They're supposed to change when they get there. None of them take any notice. They just cover up with a coat. The managers turn a blind eye.

'You're home then, Rob,' she says, checking her watch.

Dad looks round, trying to be the comedian. 'Looks like it,' he says when she ignores him.

The half-hearted attempt at humour might work better if he didn't say the same thing every single day, but that's Dad. He used to be a parrot, but he's all right now, all right now, all right now.

'You're in time to drop Lauren off at dance,' Mum tells him. 'Oh, and I said you'd pick up Katie on the way.'

Dad's expression changes. I can almost feel the charge arcing through the air.

'Come on,' Mum says. 'Don't pull a face.'

'It's uncomfortable,' Dad says. 'You know, after what happened.' Briefly, his eyes flick towards me.

'Life goes on,' Mum says, 'and Lauren and Katie get on really well. Rob, they're in the same year at school. You can't just ask them to stop seeing each other. They've become best friends since Florida.'

I know Dad wants to say more, but Lauren's still around so he lets it pass. It's time for me to make like the Cheshire Cat and vanish. I don't go far though. I want to be around when Dad comes back for a second bite of the cherry, as I know he will. It's only a couple of minutes before he intercepts her on the way out of the door.

'I can't believe you've put me in this position,' he hisses. He's out in the corridor and he thinks I can't hear him but I'm sitting on the couch by the wall. I planned it that way.

'Oh, grow up, Rob,' Mum retorts. 'You don't mind *me* picking Katie up. You don't mind Annie going round there babysitting either. It's OK for us to be uncomfortable, I suppose.'

That's right, I've been babysitting for the Sorrels a couple of times, which is how I found John's diary.

'I'd rather none of us had anything to do with that family,' Dad says.

'Listen to yourself, Rob. The Sorrels aren't bad people. They're victims. They've suffered a tragedy. Suicide isn't catching, you know. You don't pick it up from toilet seats.'

That's when Dad comes out with it. 'It isn't normal, either. What makes a lad of sixteen take his own life, tell me that? There's got to be something seriously wrong with that family.'

Mum's impatience comes seeping through the walls. 'That's a terrible thing to say, Rob. We made friends with them on holiday. Are you seriously trying to blame them for what happened? He was being bullied, Rob. Those kids at school made his life a misery. Don't you remember what it was like to be a kid?'

Dad isn't going to be persuaded that easily. 'I got a bit of skitting, the odd fight. Goes with the territory. It never did me any harm.'

Yes, he really does say that. I'm not making it up.

'For goodness' sake, Penny,' he continues, 'everyone goes through it. It's a rite of passage.'

'Just because it happens, doesn't mean it's right,' Mum retorts. 'I think these kids overstepped the mark. It wasn't just your usual name-calling. John was a sensitive boy. He couldn't cope.'

Dad sticks to his guns. 'The police didn't find any evidence of bullying.'

That brings another sigh from Mum. 'Oh, and that means it didn't happen? Kids clam up over things like that. I believe the family. Look, tragedies happen in good families too. There but for fortune go any of us. Who knows what went on in that

25

young man's mind? It was his mocks. Some youngsters really struggle with the stress of exams.'

'Behave,' Dad says. 'He ran rings round the rest of us. Penny, the lad was a virtual genius. He would have sailed through his exams.'

'Doesn't mean he didn't feel the pressure,' Mum argues. 'Even the brightest kids have nerves.'

I can feel her give Dad an exasperated stare. 'Oh, who knows? Look, anything could have pushed him over the edge. Teenagers can be very vulnerable.'

Dad takes a deep breath. 'What about, Annie?' he says. 'I'm worried about the effect on her. It's not good for her, all this. She's got her exams coming up and all she can think about is what happened to John. It's as if she's taking the blame. It's affecting her. Wouldn't it be better for all of us if we had a bit less to do with the Sorrels?'

Mum comes back, as brittle as ice on a puddle. 'Fine,' she says, 'your protest's noted but I've promised Katie a lift and that's all there is to it. Now, can I go to work?'

Dad doesn't leave it at that. I can see them out of the window now. He's caught up with her by the front gate and given her a kiss. She's kissing him back, squeezing his arm to reassure him. He doesn't like them parting in a bad mood. I'm thankful for that. I know they'll always make up. Whenever I feel down, whenever every cloud in the sky seems to have an inky black lining, they're always there, Mum and Dad. Yes, I know it's fashionable to slag your parents off, but mine, well, they're great. They're my emotional safety net. I'm not sure there was anyone to catch John when he fell and he must have been falling a long, long while by the time I met him. His wings were all burned and the sea was rushing towards him. I don't blame his mum. She's nice, if a bit highly strung. She's a small woman, very pale and fragile-looking. There's something out of kilter in that house, though. Dad's got that right. Whenever Mr Sorrel walks in the room his wife seems to shrink, to fold up inside herself and crumple. That's where John got it from, I suppose: his fear of the world. OK, maybe I'm exaggerating, things aren't like that all

26

the time. Katie's fine, a really bubbly little girl. Over in Florida Mr and Mrs Sorrel could be quite touchy-feely at times. Then something would happen, always to do with John, and things would turn sour.

'Come on, poppet,' Dad calls, putting my thoughts to flight.

He's talking to Lauren, not me. I've grown out of poppet. I catch my reflection in the mirror. Yes, I'm definitely an ex-poppet. He's ready to run her to her dance class.

'Have you got any homework?' he asks me on the way out.

'Yes, IT,' I tell him. 'I've got a PowerPoint presentation to do.'

'What, first day back?'

'Uh-huh, but our next lesson isn't till Monday.'

'Better get down to it though, hadn't you?' Dad says. 'No sense leaving it until the last minute.'

He's big on education, my dad, mainly because his wasn't too good. He couldn't settle to anything when he was younger and now he thinks it's too late. So we don't go the same way as him, he wants Lauren and me to be twenty-four-carat geniuses. We're talking brain surgeon, solicitor, research scientist, that sort of thing, not a PC doctor in a retail park.

'I'll get it done,' I say. 'When do I ever forget?'

'I know,' he says. 'You're a star. I was just checking. That's what parents do. It's our job.'

'No probs,' I say. 'I'm on to it.'

I'm already sitting at the computer when the car doors slam and the engine throbs into the night. I stare at the screen for a long while before I press the power button. Starting my homework is a reminder, if I needed one, that tomorrow's another school day. The boys will be there. I think about John and my promise to bring him justice.

from John's diary
Tuesday, 15th April

I went on Terror Tower today and I wasn't scared (well, I didn't show it!). I had Annie with me.

While the others were queuing for a second go, a second stomach-churning free-fall, I offered to get the drinks. At the back of my mind I suppose I was hoping they'd reach the front of the queue before I got back. If I wanted to be dropped down a shaft I'd have been born a stone. Anyway, I waited in the sun for 20 minutes and I didn't get fed up. My neck was starting to burn but I didn't mind. Annie came with me.

I know she's probably only being friendly. It isn't going to be more than that, is it? What girl is going to want to be with me? Let's face it, I'm not much of a specimen to show off to your friends. But we're hanging out together and she doesn't look one bit embarrassed. She laughs a lot, and I mean *with* me not *at* me.

When we got back with the drinks Mum said we were real heroes waiting all that while in the sun. I like being a hero. But I'm only a hero when Annie's around. The rest of the time I'm me.

I've got to admit I was dreading this fortnight. The pressure is always on then. I have to enter the Fun Zone, whether I want to or not. Stress Hound wants Katie and me to show we're enjoying ourselves, and I mean *show* it. If he doesn't get a big toothy grin in every frame of video, then you're just not trying. He wants his money's worth and that means fun you can see, fun you can touch, fun you can record, fun that will light up his declining years when he's old and grey. Oh yes, we're talking fun for posterity here, fun you keep stored in a row of cassettes on a shelf in the living room. Katie always comes up with the goods. I think she was born posing. Stress Hound's got her hugging Mickey, kissing Goofy, getting

28

autographs from Winnie the Pooh and Eeyore and a couple of miscellaneous mammals I'm not sure about. Jessica was the same before she went to Coventry. She was the life and soul of the party, too. There are still four videos of her dance performances at home. It's different with me. You'd be surprised how many photos there are of me frowning or looking down at the ground. It's my speciality, the downcast look. It drives Stress Hound crazy. He can't stand it.

'For God's sake, John, cheer up,' he said last night. 'One of these days I'm going to staple a smile to that miserable face.'

He's got a cheek. If he wants me to smile, why can't he, just for once, say something nice to me? Every time he comes near I feel as though I'm supposed to apologise. Sorry, Dad. Sorry for being the wrong kind of son. Sorry for being me. Sorry for every lousy thing I am. But I smile when I'm with Annie. She's so easy to talk to. She listens. How could I ever have thought Bryony was the one I was interested in?

The day flew. It was over in the blink of an eye. Then Katie, clever, wonderful Katie, begged the Chapmans to come back to the villa with us. All these years I've thought she was a pain in the neck and here she is, finding a way to keep Annie by my side.

Stress Hound and Mr Chapman, Rob, went out for potato salad and fried chicken. Katie and Lauren got the CD player working. Next thing you know they're playing some stupid track and shaking their bottoms, their *booties* – that's the technical word for it. It wasn't long before Annie joined in. She even got me to do it. I tried to hang back but Annie has a way of getting you involved. When Stress Hound and Rob walked in we were all doing it.

That's when Stress Hound said it. 'It'll do you good, John, work off some of that flab.'

It was one of those silent moments, tumbleweeds rolling through the living room, wind whistling mournfully in the trees. That must mean everybody thought he was being horrible to me. Mum did. I could see it in her eyes. She didn't stand up for me though. With every fibre of my being, I was willing her to. I wanted her to throw Dad's stupid jibe back in his face. I imagined her sweeping out of the door, taking me with her and leaving Stress Hound on his own, looking stupid. I could hear the voice in my

29

head. Please, you're my mum. Please. Instead she just sat there wilting, giving in to the old get as usual. Well, hello there Agony Kitten, welcome back, welcome back, welcome back.

That moment, the walls of the world fell in on me. I hated myself for daring to have fun, daring to forget I was the Lardy Boy. I didn't even look at him. I stamped out to the pool and sat on one of the loungers, burning up inside, neck prickling at the picture in my head of my pathetic, lardy backside quivering like jelly.

I could smell the chicken but I wasn't going to walk in and get any with Stress Hound there. I'd have been sick. Yes, one word from him and I would have vomited everywhere, a technicolour yawn all over my moronic father.

Agony Kitten came out with some food but I shook my head. Why couldn't she understand? I needed her to know how bad I felt, how Stress Hound had spoiled the moment. OK, so she couldn't come out against him openly, but there were other things she could do. I wanted her to say something, to squeeze my shoulder, to make me feel better. She didn't.

She left some chicken and a plate of potato salad. Much as I wanted to shovel it in, feel the grease running down my chin, the comfort in my gut, I let it sit there. I wanted Stress Hound to see me, registering my protest, but I could hear him indoors, laughing about something. As usual he'd forgotten it had ever happened. I could sulk all night and it wouldn't shame him. Him and goldfish, same attention span, three seconds. I'm the one who's left with the bad taste in my mouth.

After about five minutes somebody joined me. It was Annie. She sat on the end of the lounger and put her hand on my knee. I swear, I very nearly jumped out of my skin. The touch of her hand on my flesh was like an electric charge. No way was I going to ask her to move it. I liked it there. I liked the sudden cool of her fingers on my burning skin. When she took her hand away I could still feel the brush of her fingertips and longed for her to touch me again. So many years I've wanted someone to touch me that way.

'Take no notice,' Annie said. 'Dads are like that.'

'Yours isn't.'

'No,' Annie said. 'He isn't. You shouldn't take it to heart though.

I'm sure he didn't mean to hurt your feelings. Some guys, they're just a bit thick-skinned.'

'Yes?' I said, heavy on the sarcasm. 'And what makes you so sure he didn't mean it?'

'Men do it all the time,' she said. 'Look at the lads in school. They're always winding somebody up. It's what they do.'

My face must have changed because she followed up with: 'You don't like that sort of thing, do you?'

I shook my head. 'No.'

'So do you get picked on yourself?'

I nodded. Is ice cream cold? 'You never noticed, then, at school?'

Annie shook her head. 'It's a big place.'

She must have thought that was a bit lame because she added: 'We didn't know each other that well, did we?'

Another shake of the head. 'No, we didn't.'

How does that happen? Every day of my lousy life I've got Woodford, Rice and their scummy mates cutting me, bruising me, making me wish I was dead and nobody else knows, not even this beautiful, understanding girl who's sitting next to me trying to help. Sometimes they'd follow me round all day calling me Joanne. Stupid I know, but after five and a half hours it gets to you. How can the others fail to notice what's going on? I want to scream and scream until my throat bleeds and yet the whole world goes on as normal around me. There's just me with my head pinned in an invisible vice being slowly crushed. Still, nobody sees. It's as though everybody carries on their lives walled up inside themselves and all those other lives circling around them, all that pain and hurt, just bounces off. They don't even know it's there.

'Is it bad?'

I answer with a nod. Sometimes words fail you. They hit the sharp edges of life and they lose all shape. Meaning breaks apart. Here was Annie wanting to understand and I had no way of getting it across, just how much I hated what they put me through.

'Oh, it's bad.'

'So what do they do to you?'

I sigh. This is the trouble. Nobody understands. Given time, a lot of small stones become an avalanche. A few flakes of low-level

31

teasing make a blizzard of hurt in the end. I've tried to explain to Mum. Sometimes, after one of our conversations, she's all fired-up and ready to take on the world. She's all set to go into school and have it out with Mr Storey. So many times I've come away from one of our talks walking on air, thinking at last something's going to be done. I dare to dream that, maybe this time, it will all be over. But every time Stress Hound manages to talk her out of it, persuade her it'll only make things worse, that it's best to let it run its course. Then all that hope, all those dreams of living a normal life crumble.

'John,' Annie says again, 'what do they do?'

'It'll sound stupid.'

But Annie had an answer. 'You don't know how it will sound until you say it.'

'There's a lot of name-calling, skitting . . .'

'What about?'

'What do you think? They say I'm fat, same as Stress Hound does.'

Annie laughs. 'Stress Hound, is that your dad?'

I nod and Annie touches me again. This time she reaches for my hand. It's going dark now and nobody's put the pool lights on. We're sitting among the shadows and the sub-tropical dusk.

'You're not fat,' Annie says. 'You're fine.'

Wrong, I'm John Sorrel trapped in this lousy fat kid body. 'I'm not fine.'

'Why, what's wrong with you?'

'Well, I'm certainly not thin, am I?' I reply. 'My own dad makes fun of my size. The kids at school are the same. I've tried diets. Always on the look out for the magic formula, that's me. I tear them out of Mum's magazines. I've tried points and no-carbs and fruit days and all that crap, one after the other. None of them work. You know I starved myself once for two whole days, throwing my meals away when nobody was looking. Trouble is, I pigged out after that and made it worse than ever. It's in my genes, I guess.'

Annie frowns. 'Who told you that?' she asks. 'Both your parents are slim.'

She's right, so how come I put it on so easily?

'Let those boys call you fat,' Annie says. 'You know you're not. Ignore them.'

32

I have another stab at explaining. 'It doesn't work like that. They say it all the time. They say it over and over again. They wouldn't say it if it wasn't true. I look in the mirror and that's all I see, the fat kid with the moon face.'

'John,' Annie says. 'It's not true.'

'It is,' I insist. 'I'm fat. I feel like I am. They shove me around in the changing rooms, push me under the showers, hide my stuff.'

'What else?'

Oh, Annie, I can't tell you what else.

'They stand behind me when I'm on the computer, flicking me with their fingers. They follow me round all the time.'

I wait a beat before I finish it. Go on, tell her.

'They call me girls' names. They say I'm gay.'

Annie shakes her head. 'They're so stupid. You've got to ignore them.'

'Easier said than done,' I tell her. I remember one time, just before the end of term. They got me in a corner and pinned me down. Then they were smearing lipstick all over me, saying if my name was Joanne, I ought to make an effort to look pretty. They called it: doing up the poof. My flesh crawls at the thought of it. I can feel the make-up, slick on my skin, the lipstick slashed across my mouth and even my teeth. I can feel myself crying inside. Any time, night or day, when I close my eyes, I find myself reliving that moment. I want to tell Annie, but nobody's that honest. Nobody wants to bathe publicly in the dirty water of their own humiliation.

'How long's this been going on?' Annie asks.

'They've never liked me much,' I say, 'but the last couple of years it's been really bad. I don't know why, maybe something to do with hitting our teens. Now all I ever hear is *fat kid, gay boy.*'

'You're not fat and you're not gay,' she says. 'Don't let it get to you, John. Just think how dumb it all is. Ignore them. They're pathetic.'

I look at her. 'How do you know I'm not gay?' I ask. 'We've only just made friends.'

Her eyes meet mine. We look at each other that way for a long time.

'John,' she says finally, forced by my silence to explain herself. 'I've seen the way you look at me. Believe me, you're not gay.'

33

Annie's right, of course. I'm not gay. It might make it easier if I were. At least I'd have an idea why they're doing it. But I'm not. Useless with girls is what I am. Stuck with a big fat tongue that can't do chat-up is what I am. Yes, and a big fat body too. I got a leaflet a few months back, Teen Gym. I went along, just the once, but all the other kids were really skinny. None of them needed the gym. I stuck out like a sore thumb. I knew what they were all thinking: what's the fat kid doing here? I never went back. Crazy, isn't it? If you're fat you need to go and work out. But if you're fat, you're too self-conscious to even start. Catch 22.

If I could only talk to a girl like other lads, if I could just get a girl to get to know me . . . But that's what Annie's doing, isn't it? She talks to me, smiles at me. She looks at me too. The way she looked at me tonight, it made my throat dry. Her gaze was long and hard, as though there was a real connection between us. Am I hoping for too much? Am I wishing too hard? I won't get to know, not for a couple of days at least. The Chapmans are going over to the Gulf Coast. Mum and Stress Hound have managed to persuade Katie that we're going to an Outlet Mall. I get to see Annie again Thursday. I'm already counting the hours.

Glass

Glass breaks
because it is fragile.
You don't blame
the glass
for breaking.
A heart breaks
because it is fragile.
So why blame
the heart
for breaking?
Why blame me?

Annie

Sunday, 7th September

It was towards the end of the first week when John started to open up to me. He told me about the bullying. It sounded like the usual stuff, the stuff you read about in the newspapers or hear about in assembly: name-calling, a bit of push and shove, leaving you out of the loop. He used to get teased for being bright. With some kids, it isn't cool to have a brain. Not that I took it all that seriously at first. It's hard when you've never had any problem with bullying. I wouldn't say I was the life and soul of the party but I did OK. I had plenty of friends.

I haven't been aware of any bullying around school either. A couple of times at primary school this or that girl would leave me out of a game, but I didn't let it get to me all that much. I was stronger than that. People are spiteful sometimes. They go off on one. It's not what you'd strictly call bullying. A quiet cry in a corner and I was over it. It must have got to me from time to time but I don't remember being upset for very long. I took it in my stride.

Then along came Bryony. From the day she arrived at junior school, in Year Five, we were pretty much inseparable. From that moment on, when it came to any bitchiness (weird how, after all this politically correct stuff, there doesn't seem a better word for the way some girls behave), I was fireproof. I had Bryony to fall back on. I could tell her anything. She was every friend I could ever have wanted.

But why didn't I take John seriously about the bullying? I don't know really. It's never happened to me, so maybe I didn't recognise the signs. I couldn't understand why he didn't stand up for himself. He was capable of it. There was that time at

36

Disney. I saw John stand up to somebody, really stand up. I suppose I thought, if he can do it there, why not back home? We'd been getting drinks. I think John only did it to avoid going on Terror Tower again. Anyway, we were standing behind this guy and his son, a kid four, maybe five, years old. The kid was grizzling about being hot and thirsty. After five minutes of this, the father started dragging the kid round by the hand, telling him to shut up. OK, so the average fractious five-year-old can be pretty unappealing, all slippery with snot and tears, but his father lost it big time. The kid tumbled over and scraped his knees. Suddenly he was bawling his head off. That made his Dad worse. He got red in the face and started smacking the kid's legs, every slap just making the kid wail and howl louder and louder, which is when John did it. Out of the blue, he spoke up:

'You probably think I'm interfering, sir,' he said.

I thought that was a nice touch. Sir. Very American. Like he respected the moron. He continued in the same tone, calm and even.

'But your son's hot and fed up,' John said, 'that's all. Can't you try to be patient?'

Just like that, he said it, quiet and restrained, but firm. He was so mature. The man was in no mood to listen, of course, not in mid-slap. He glared at John and said something under his breath. It wasn't the kind of word you find in the Bible, let's put it like that. A couple of minutes later though, when he'd got the drinks, he bent down and dabbed the kid's tears with a hankie. Then he hugged his son. I think he was quite close to tears himself. That's when he stole a glance at John. The look was full of pain and humiliation, but there was something else. It was a silent apology, to John and the little boy. I felt so proud of my friend then, my sweet, quiet, brave John.

So why, if he could stand up for that little kid, did he never stand up for himself? That's what keeps nagging away at me. Maybe I don't understand how deep it went, this hurt that he felt. He told me what the boys did to him but, though I listened sympathetically enough, I didn't for one moment put myself in his shoes. To me, it was a long list of petty incidents. To him it was Hell.

Even when he showed me his poems I didn't get it. They made me feel uncomfortable more than anything. I mean, if somebody bares their soul, shouldn't they do it in private? All this stuff about pain and hurt, about being broken inside, it was too personal, too downright bleak. For the first time since I met him I started feeling impatient. Though it sounds terrible in light of what happened, it actually crossed my mind he might be putting it on. Could John be a bit of an attention-seeker?

But John wasn't putting anything on. Nothing was made up, or over-exaggerated. I understand that now. All those things he told me, they really did carve him open. All those feelings he wrote about, they were real. There was that much darkness in his life. That's what I find so hard to take. Brick by brick, stone by stone, the citadel in which John lived was dismantled. Still, no matter what he did or said, nobody took any notice. All they did was stand around while it happened. That goes for John's family. Yes, it goes for me too. That, when it comes right down to it, is why I have to do this for him. From somewhere I have to find the strength to speak up for him. I have to get Woodford, Rice and the others to take a long, hard look at themselves. They've got to admit their guilt.

Whenever I start thinking about tomorrow, whenever I imagine their faces, I feel sick to the pit of my stomach. Those first few days in school, I suppose I can make excuses for not doing anything. I hadn't settled in. I was unsure of myself. After my year abroad, it was like starting over. But if I let it run on, if I go, day after day, week after week, without saying anything then I really am letting John down. I'm letting him die all over again. I'm still thinking this way when Bryony phones.

'Hey you,' she says.

That's her usual starter for ten.

'Hey you,' I say back. 'Am I forgiven?'

'What for?'

'You know, my fit of the heavies last week. I think I got a bit intense.'

There is just the hint of a pause but she says what I want to hear. 'Don't be daft. There's nothing to forgive. Do you want to go down the Mega-Bowl tonight?'

'Who's going?'

'Joanne, Shobna, Kelly, the usual posse.'

This is just what I need, a good old girls' night out. 'OK, why not?'

'Great, my dad will give us a lift down.'

'What about getting picked up afterwards?' I ask, thinking ahead to what my parents will say. They're pretty traditional, in by ten during the week, eleven at the weekend.

'Mum's working,' I explain. 'Dad might offer. Depends how long we're staying out.'

I'm about to go into the details of Lauren's bedtime when Bryony interrupts.

'You're OK. Dad will drop you back off at home too.'

So, come seven o'clock, I'm in Bryony's car. Joanne and Shobna are getting a lift too, so the decibel level is going through the roof. Kelly is meeting us there. This is the first time I've been out with friends since I came home and I'm nervous. The Mega-Bowl isn't just about bowling. It's about copping off. Last time I came – OK, it was a year ago but you don't forget these things easily – everybody ended up talking to a boy except me. I had to play gooseberry for three-quarters of an hour, trying not to look bothered. Yes, it's a good trick if you can do it, standing there with a big, plastic grin on your face looking completely uncon- cerned while your stomach dissolves with disappointment and humiliation. I've never been so glad to see Dad.

At the Mega-Bowl we bail out, hurrying over the rain-slicked pavements. Bryony gets the dos and don'ts from her Dad, and the usual multiple reminder of when he'll pick us up. The moment his brake lights flare at the end of the car park Bryony gives a meaningful giggle and we go inside. Shobna's the one who booked the lanes so she goes over to sort things out while we look around. Joanne says something about a boy in Lane 5.

'No way,' says Kelly. 'He took me to the Odeon a few weeks ago. We're talking first degree halitosis.'

'Hali-what?' says Joanne.

She knows what it is, but she thinks it's cool to be dumb.

'Halitosis, sprouts-for-brains. It means bad breath.'

'You've snogged him, then?' says Bryony, a wicked little smile spreading across her face.

Kelly screws her eyes up the way she does and everybody laughs, even me. Halitosis Boy sees Kelly and waves. When we burst out laughing his forehead rumples into a frown. That's his self-esteem knocked for six. I can't help thinking of John.

'What do you think of them?' he asked, the night he showed me his poems. 'I've never shown them to anyone else.'

Not knowing quite what to say, I answered with a question of my own. 'What makes you write poetry?'

'I write it for me,' he said, 'to try to put the way I feel into words. That's the way it is with poetry, it's a kind of excavation. You dig down, find out what's in the lower levels of yourself.'

Then I asked another question. 'And if you were writing for someone else,' I said, 'what would you want them to feel?'

'Pain,' John said simply, 'I'd want them to feel my pain.'

He went on to explain. One PE lesson Woodford grabbed John from behind and started telling everybody he had boobs and he needed a bra. Then the Gang of Four had him on the floor trying to put one on him. It's hard to credit, but Luke had actually brought one of his sister's in. This wasn't spur of the moment. He planned it. Imagine that, he sneaked into his sister's room to steal a bra, then brought it in his bag. Weird, or what!

'I fought them,' John said. 'I really fought them. It was so bad I cracked a tooth.'

'And nobody told the teachers?' I asked.

John shook his head. 'My mate Peter wanted to, but Woodford asked him if he wanted the same treatment and that shut him up. I even lied to Mum about it. It was months before she found out how I really broke my tooth.'

John had tears in his eyes talking about it. I remember regretting I had ever asked.

That's when I hear Bryony's voice, breaking in on the past. 'Penny for them.'

'I beg your pardon.'

'Your thoughts,' she explains. 'A penny for your thoughts. You were miles away.'

'Oh, sorry.'

'Have you seen who's looking at you?' Kelly says.

'Who?'

'Only Matthew Rice, gorgeous hunk of this parish.'

My neck blisters with a rash of heat. John said Woodford was the ring-leader but Matthew had to be there too.

'Don't make fun of me,' I tell her.

'Who's making fun? He's been staring since we came in.'

I shrug it off but when I steal a glance he's looking all right. Oh God, Matthew Rice looking at me. My heart is jumping like a toad. It's not with excitement though, the way it would have been a year ago. I feel like gagging. Matthew Rice, tormentor; Matthew Rice, killer, and he is looking at me.

'Can we just bowl?' I say.

Kelly shakes her head. 'If Matthew was looking at me, bowling would be the last thing on my mind.'

Shobna's back. 'Change your shoes, girls,' she says.

For a few minutes I'm lost in it all: the crash of the bowling balls, the thumping music, the rhythm of conversation and laughter. I could almost believe I don't have a mission. But that's not true. A boy is dead and I have to get justice for him. Ten minutes later it's my turn to go for drinks. I pay and turn to go. Guess what? There's Matthew Rice blocking my way. Why now? Why here?

'Excuse me, please,' I say.

Please. To him. To this creature.

'It's Annie, isn't it?' Matthew says. 'Where've you been . . .?'

'What, all your life?' I say, interrupting.

I'm surprised at myself. It's not like me to be sarcastic but this is Matthew Rice. I can be as flip and cruel as I want. He deserves it. He flinches visibly but ploughs on.

'I was going to say, since last year. You just vanished off the face of the earth.'

Matthew Rice! He noticed *me*. Oh, listen to yourself, Annie.

Don't tell me you're flattered by that cockroach. Just a minute though. He can't have been that keen. He didn't notice enough to ask around after me. Bryony would soon have told him where I'd gone if he'd asked her.

'My dad was working overseas,' I say. What am I doing? Why am I exchanging small talk? I should be telling him what I think of him. I should be standing up for John, poor, gentle John who never hurt a fly and was broken by Matthew Rice and the rest of the pack hounds.

'Anywhere interesting?'

Now my flesh is crawling. Say something, *anything*, stop acting like a wuss.

'Look, Matthew,' I say. 'I've got to get back to my friends.'

I glance in their direction. Oh great, they're pointing and talking behind their hands, like something out of a teen-flick. They're still living in a normal world where I'm flattered by this boy's attention.

'I'm sure you can spare me a minute,' he says, giving me a quiet smile that says: you're impressed with me, I know you are.

Listen to you, Matthew. You really do love yourself, don't you? Flustered, all I can do is repeat myself. 'I've got to get back.'

There's a shake in my voice. I can hear it and Matthew would have to be deaf or stupid, or both, not to hear it himself.

'Have I done something to upset you?' he asks, the top coat flaking off his smile.

Has he done something? I can see John lying face down on the changing room floor with them all laughing at him. I can feel all his shame and helplessness. Yes, me, who's never had any problems in school, suddenly I understand what it must have been like, how he must have been on edge every minute of every day. That's when I say it. That's when I finally speak up.

'You shouldn't be asking me that. You should be asking John Sorrel.'

Moments later, I'm in the loo with Bryony, Kelly and Shobna, and we're not talking make-up.

42

'What the hell happened out there?' Shobna asks. 'What made him kick off like that?'

'Yes,' Kelly said, excited. 'Tell all.'

I wouldn't say Matthew Rice *kicked off* exactly. He surprised me. I don't know what I expected: anger, protests of innocence, panic even. But he froze. That's what he did. He froze. Then he grabbed me by the shoulders. He wasn't angry or threatening in any way. The way he held me was similar to the way John held me in Florida, like a shipwrecked sailor clinging to a raft. Then, very loudly, he said: 'Repeat that.'

I wouldn't call it a shout. It was more a moan that came from somewhere deep inside him. It was as though he had been slapped in the face and he wanted to know why. I wouldn't say everybody turned to stare. That would have been impossible with the music blaring. But enough people turned to make me self-conscious.

'John Sorrel,' I told him. 'You should ask John Sorrel why I'm upset.' Then the follow-up. 'Oh no,' I said, very coolly, with a presence of mind that surprised me. 'He can't answer, can he?'

I let a beat of silence follow while the blood drained from Matthew's face, then I hit him with the follow-through.

'He's dead.'

People probably heard what Matthew said. I don't think they will have heard me. I said it quietly, but deliberately. I didn't plan on making a scene. I just wanted him to think about what he'd done. Time seemed to shudder to a halt. For long moments Matthew didn't say a word. The only sign of life was his Adam's apple working up and down. Then, when I thought he must have turned into a pillar of salt or something, he spoke.

'You're crazy,' he said, spinning on his heel and walking away in the direction of his friends.

Then, once more, as he reached them, he repeated: 'Crazy.'

'Well,' Bryony says. 'What happened with Matthew?'

The question sounds different coming from her. Unlike the others, she knows what it's all about. She is apprehensive, not excited.

'He tried to chat me up,' I say.

43

'Matthew Rice! No way!'

'What did you say?'

I catch Bryony's eye. She's desperate for me to keep my little secret under my hat.

'I told him to leave me alone.'

'You did what!'

Kelly is stunned. Joanne too.

'You said no to Matthew Rice! We're talking Orlando Bloom's younger brother, Adonis. You've got to be crazy.'

I shake my head. 'That's what Matthew said.'

Joanne, Kelly and Shobna lead the way outside still talking about my act of madness.

Bryony hangs behind. 'Thanks,' she says.

'For what?'

'For not making a scene.'

I almost burst out laughing. 'It was a bit of a scene.'

'All right then,' Bryony says, 'thanks for not making more of a scene.'

'It's going to come out, you know, what I said to him.'

Bryony sighs. 'I know.'

'And you'll still be my friend?'

We're by the lanes now. I don't see Matthew.

'You know I will,' Bryony says. 'Friends for keeps. It doesn't mean I like all this.'

The others are calling us.

'You don't have to like it,' I say. 'You just have to understand.'

Bryony is still wearing her troubled look. Understand? I'm not one bit sure she does.

The evening isn't over, and Matthew hasn't gone. Things come back to haunt me as we stand outside waiting for Bryony's dad. It's Luke Woodford. Matthew is standing in the doorway. He looks like a little boy who's lost his Game Boy. Michael Okey's hovering too. There's no sign of Anthony Fraser.

'Have you got something to say?' Luke demands.

He's walking quickly. For a moment I think he's going to march straight up to me and slap me. I see the dark shine in his eyes. It's pure rage. His jaw clenches. The veins throb in his temples and his face flushes deep red. When I said what I did to Matthew I had him on the back foot. It isn't like that with Luke. Defence isn't his game. The person isn't born who has Luke on the back foot. I've seen him drive teachers to distraction, not by doing anything particularly outrageous, but by keeping up the drip-drip-drip of hostility. And can he do hostile!

'I've nothing to say to you,' I tell him.

It's not true. I've got a lot to say to him. Not here though, not in a rain-swept car park on a blowy autumn evening when I haven't given any thought to what I want to say. Right now I'm too scared. Every instinct tells me to back off. I can see Bryony and the others flashing glances at each other. The whole thing is spiralling out of control.

'You were happy enough shooting your mouth off before,' Luke says. 'So if you've something to say, come right out with it. I'm waiting.'

It sounds like he's criticising Matthew somehow, calling him a wimp or something for letting me get to him. Luke's standing in front of me, oblivious to the others. He's got his fists bunched by his sides, though I know he won't hit me. He's got other ways to hurt. Still, things have gone too far for me to clam up. Much as I want to, I can't hide from this. Finally the words come.

'I didn't say anything that isn't true.'

The veins in his forehead bulge again. 'Yes? And how would you know? You weren't even here.'

I can feel Bryony tugging at my sleeve, trying to prise me away but, scared as I am, I have to answer back.

'I saw John in America. He told me all about you.' My voice falters. There's a fine rain falling, sprinkling my face with pixels of cold. 'What you did . . . what you said.'

Luke's eyes stay on me. They are steady, unfazed. His look bores right inside me.

'The coppers grilled us about all this,' he says with a sneer. 'We came up clean.'

No, I decide, I'm not backing down. 'Just because they didn't find any dirt,' I retort, 'doesn't mean you're clean.'

45

Bryony is still clinging to my sleeve. I was glad of her presence at first. Suddenly I don't need her any more. Nothing Luke can do is going to scare me.

'You know what you did, Luke. So do I. You're going to pay.'

Car headlights illuminate the group, the diamond shards of the raindrops flashing. It's Bryony's dad. Luke's gaze shifts to the driver.

'Is that right? So who's going to make me?'

He follows me almost to the car door. 'You're going to make me pay, are you? I wouldn't bet on it.'

from John's diary
Thursday, 17th April

The day got off to a bad start. Katie caught me standing in front of the mirror, sucking my belly in, trying to torture myself thin. Lots of people must do this kind of thing, trying to see another slimmer, better, self reflected in the glass. They get what I got, grim confirmation that, yes, they are as big as they thought. But that's not me. There's more to me than the fat kid who stares back from the mirror. I've got feelings. I've got all sorts of hopes and dreams. I won a creative writing competition before Christmas. My story was published in the *Excellence in Cities* magazine. You know what the other kids said? They called me a creep. They hated me for brown-nosing the teachers. Why don't people listen to what you say? Why don't they take notice of what you do? Why's it always how you look and whether you fit in? I don't want to play rap and wear a baseball cap back to front. I don't want to hang around in the street all night. You know what I want: I want to be left alone.

Anyway, back to our Katie. For the next half hour – or maybe it was only a few minutes; it *felt* like half an hour – she was prancing round the house blowing out her cheeks and sucking in a stomach she doesn't have. Do I hate anorexic dwarves from Hell – or sisters, as they are more commonly called.

'John's making himself beautiful,' she started singing. 'John loves himself.'

I tried swatting her with a magazine, but that only made her worse. A human wasp, that's what she is.

'John loves himself, John loves himself, but . . . '

Don't you dare, I thought.

'. . . he loves his Annie more.'

I tried to shut her up. It didn't work. It never does. When Katie's got a bee in her bonnet she goes on, and on . . .

'Oh, knock it off, you little worm,' I complained. Wasps, bees, worms, I'm a right little zoologist today!

'John loves himself, but he loves his Annie more.'

. . . and on!

Stress Hound took advantage of the moment. Of course he did.

'You too can have a body like mine,' he jibed. 'If you don't take care of yourself.'

Well, gee, thanks for the usual vote of confidence, Dad. Never miss a trick, do you?

'Leave the lad alone, Phil,' Mum said.

Hear that? Not even: *leave him alone, he's not fat.* She couldn't even muster that much conviction.

'He's got to learn to take a bit of ribbing,' Stress Hound retorted. 'You don't want him growing up soft.'

No, God forbid, that would never do, would it? Phil Sorrel's son, the soft kid, the fat boy, the lardy lad. We've all got to be hard, haven't we? Men made of wood and plastic, that's what we want. Yes, meet Teflon Man, the feelings run right off him.

'John loves his Annie more,' Katie chanted.

'Katie,' Mum said, 'that will do.'

But Katie's right. The whole of yesterday, all I did was think of Annie. I've had crushes before. I've written girls' names in my jotter, imagined my lips against theirs, even trailed round after them once or twice until they noticed. But this is different. There is actually something there between us. This isn't daydreaming. It isn't fantasy.

Now I was going to see her again and I was dreading it. It's *where* I was seeing her that made my throat go tight. We were going to meet the Chapmans at Blizzard Beach, one of the Disney water parks. Stress Hound's idea.

It's all right for Stress Hound. It doesn't bother him, taking his shirt off. He's got sallow skin and well-defined muscles, and the whole thing is covered in a mat of dark hair. It doesn't even bother him that he's going bald.

'Pity I can't graft some from down here,' he'll say, running his hands over the carpet of hair on his chest.

He has a number two crop and he looks fine, the very picture of bullet-headed masculinity. I wish I took after him, but I have to have Mum's pale, pasty features. Trouble is, instead of being pale, pasty and thin like her I have to be pale, pasty and fat. Genetically, I'm a wimp.

All the way down Highway 192 I was dreading it, taking my shirt off in front of Annie. Then I would have Mum faffing and fussing over me, insisting I slicked on multiple layers of Factor 35. White, blubbery *and* slippery. Now isn't that a lovely combination? Look at me, I'm the great white sausage, a bar of soap with legs. But it didn't turn out to be the nightmare I'd expected. The day didn't start well but it ended wonderfully. When I finally, reluctantly, peeled off my tee-shirt Annie just glanced up and smiled. It's not like I stopped feeling embarrassed but – amazingly – getting my kit off didn't make it worse. Seeing me stripped down to my swimming shorts didn't seem to make any difference to Annie.

'One of these days,' she said, rubbing the gooseflesh from her arms, 'I'll actually fill a swimsuit.'

She has this weird image of herself, as if she's got no shape at all. She's wrong. I've noticed the curves. She isn't the finished thing. Annie's a lot like me in some ways. She's kind of vulnerable, not really sure of herself yet.

We watched Lauren and Katie scamper off to some obstacle course they'd been going on about. Our parents seemed content to read or sun-bathe, so Annie and me, we took ourselves off. For ages we floated round the park on doughnuts, just feeling the sun on our faces, not even talking. There was no need. We were comfortable in one another's company. I wanted the moment to last for ever.

'Do you want to go on some of the slides?' she asked eventually.

'I don't fancy that big one,' I said apprehensively.

Annie gave a sympathetic smile. 'Oh, don't worry,' she said. 'I'm not one for plummeting at sixty miles an hour. Hurtling down a slide in zero seconds, completely unable to see, where's the fun in that?'

This girl, she's just too good to be true! In the end we went on a double doughnut, Annie in front, me at the back. I had my legs stretched out either side of hers. We were touching, more than we'd ever done before. I could feel the press of her body. It made

49

me burn, probably with the novelty as much as anything. All the times I'd seen lads my age getting close up with some girl and now, suddenly, it didn't seem so impossible that it could be me. Then we were rushing downhill in a cascade of screams and spray.

'Again?' I said.

If she thought I had an agenda, that I wanted to feel her against me, she wasn't saying. Who knows? Dare I believe she feels the same way I do? So we went again . . . and again.

The day passed in a haze. I think it's called happiness. I'm not familiar with the concept. We munched doughnuts – the kind you eat, not the ones you sit in – dipped in chocolate sauce. We had hot dogs and French fries in the shade of a wooden umbrella. We swam and slid and floated and glided. She even jumped on my back and got me to give her a piggyback to where our families were sitting. I didn't want it to end. It was only when Mum told me I was beginning to burn that I realised just how completely I'd forgotten my usual inhibitions. Four, maybe five hours I'd been schlepping around in nothing but my swimming shorts and I'd hardly given it a moment's thought. I'd even given up pulling in my gut. Not being ashamed of my rubber duck body. I was one person: mind, body and soul. I was comfortable with myself. I'd begun to understand what it was like to be alive.

Happy

It's when
nobody calls you names;
it's when
you don't look round corners;
it's when
you walk without fear
of another set of footsteps
falling in behind you.
It's when
Shadows are just the absence of light
not the absence of security;
It's when
Words don't have teeth;
smiles don't have daggers;
the twinkle in their eyes
isn't edged with malice.

It's when
you dare
— just once —
to be happy.

Annie
Monday, 8th September

I knew almost from day one that John fancied me. He was infatuated. He couldn't get enough of me. It was the glances, the little touches, the brushes of his arm against mine. I didn't know how to take it. I'd never been pursued this way before. The first time John touched me all I could think about was what the girls would think.

Bryony's OK, but the others! Joanne and Shobna would be appalled that I could have anything to do with the class lardo. Oh, what am I doing? I've started using their words now. I don't want to sound like them, or Kelly. If anything, she's worse. She's a virtual body fascist. But, you know what, after a while, I didn't care. I'd have been happy to be seen with him if we went back to the UK.

John made this holiday. When we started the drive down from Departure Bay, I thought the whole thing was going to be such a chore. It was Lauren's holiday, the eight-year-old's treat. I was being dragged along just because I was too young to stay home alone, then suddenly it was fun, and that was down to him. Once he relaxed, he was always telling jokes, talking about books, movies and music, going on about these silly riddles and puzzles he made up. Twice he tried to get me to read *The Da Vinci Code*. I said it wasn't my style. He was knowledgeable. He read the newspapers. He cared about things. He had his serious, quiet moments too. Who wouldn't, with what he'd been through. All in all, he was good company, a friend.

If only he'd been allowed to be himself, he would have been all right. But he never could be himself. Some days he was off in his own dream world, others he was clinging to me like a limpet.

Then there was his relationship with his dad. That stunk to high heaven. One day we went to Sea World. There was this game where you fired a water pistol at a target. Each player had to fill a column with water. The first to get to the top rang a bell and won a prize. John was reluctant to play at first, but it turned out he was really good at it. He won a Shamu cuddly toy with his first go.

'Who wants it?' he asked, eyes sparkling.

Lauren claimed it.

'Do you want one, Katie?' John asked, suddenly glowing with confidence.

That's when Mr Sorrel had to put his oar in. 'Let me show you how it's done,' he said, pushing John off the seat. 'Make way for the master. You watch me, Katie.'

John seemed to deflate visibly. As soon as Mr Sorrel took his seat he started to walk away. I chased after him. I wasn't going to let Macho Man ruin the day.

'Don't give in, John,' I told him. 'You can still win.' John looked at me doubtfully. I squeezed his arm. 'Go on.'

Taking the last remaining seat, John glanced at his father and started training the jet of water. He crouched forward, an intense look on his face. Mr Sorrel was the same, knuckles white. I started to wonder what was going on. Competition's one thing, but this was desperation. Then John's bell rang. He'd won.

'Yes!' Clutching the cuddly toy, he handed it to a delighted Katie.

'We'd better get to Shamu Stadium,' Mrs Sorrel said.

'One more game,' John said. 'For Annie.'

He won that one too, much to Mr Sorrel's disgust, and hand-ed me the toy. I hugged John and planted a kiss on his cheek. He went bright red. Funny thing about that toy, I didn't let go of it for the rest of the day. In some way I didn't understand, that day was about more than a cuddly whale. The more Mr Sorrel put John down, the more I stuck up for him. We became really close.

But . . . yes, there always is a but, was I being fair to him?

Sometime, somehow, wouldn't there be a reckoning, a fall from grace? I liked him, really liked him. I even enjoyed the physical attention. That's right, I'm no fool, I know you don't have to be in love to feel something, physically. When he was pressed up tight against my back, when his breath was warm on my neck and his lips touched my ear lobes, I felt good. For the first time ever I felt wanted by a boy. I would have kissed him then, enjoyed it too, let him fold me in his arms. But love him, be his girlfriend? More than anything, that's what he wanted from me. Love is something else entirely, and I didn't feel that way about him. He was my friend, a bit like a favourite cousin, and that was all he would ever be.

Even while we were messing about in the wave pool, even while he was staring at me with those trusting, urgent, blue eyes, I knew there would be a time when I would have to let him down gently. But that was some time away. OK, I know, I'm a coward, and being a coward I could put it off almost indefinitely. At the end of this holiday John would go back to Grovemount and his torment. I would go back to Departure Bay. Maybe, just maybe, I could defer the truth so far into the future there never would be a reckoning. I would stay in Canada. Our phone calls and e-mails would dry up. Our Easter in Florida would become a sweet, distant memory.

There is no such deferral for me today. If not at the school gates, then sometime in the school day, I will have to face my reckoning. Matthew Rice I can handle, but Luke Woodford, he's a different kettle of fish altogether. Where Matthew was taken aback, flustered, Luke was . . . what do I call it? Righteous, that's the word that comes to mind. There was no shame. He doesn't just think he's right, he *knows* it. The police cleared him. He's got nothing to answer for.

It's not over. What happened last night was the opening shot. Now I have no choice. I've taken the first step on a long journey. I will bring John justice. If ever I did think about shrinking from my mission, the time for that is past. In confronting Matthew, I made my enemies and set myself apart. I don't even know if I will have any friends on this journey. Kelly, Joanne,

Shobna, they will probably fall away. I saw the look in their eyes while I argued with Luke in the car park last night. They were willing it to go away, but that isn't going to happen. I won't let it and nor will Luke. It's Bryony I care about. If we break friends over this, then I will have paid a high price for my promise to John.

'Are you keeping your eye on the time?'

That's Dad's voice. Mum is still in bed, catching up on sleep after her late shift.

'Yes, I've got five minutes. Besides, the bus is never on time.'

'Well, don't cut it too fine,' Dad calls.

I know he will be like a cat on hot tiles until I go, so I shove my planner into my bag and head for the door.

'Going now,' I call.

'Have a nice day,' Dad shouts back.

Have a nice day, eh? Something you picked up in America, Dad? Lauren doesn't say anything. She's trying to get her lunch box in her backpack and that's taking all the concentration she's got.

Have a nice day. How nice a day I can have with the boys waiting for me is anybody's guess. But they will be waiting. Luke will see to that. It's raining outside. Pulling up my hood, I jog across the road and shelter under the dripping trees. I can feel the spray from the traffic soaking into my tights already. Come on, bus. There is a cluster of Year 9 boys at the bus stop. One of them turns and smiles, then gets a dig in the ribs from one of his mates. This is happening too often to be coincidence.

'Annie!'

A girl's voice. I look around. It's Shobna. She's sticking her head out of the passenger window of the family car.

'Get in. We'll give you a lift.'

I get a nod from Shobna's mum.

'Thanks,' I say.

I'm not really grateful. I know that, the moment we get dropped off at school, Shobna will start the third degree. I know how all the others will react, too. Kelly will be resentful. She'd like Matthew for herself. She'll think I'm queering the pitch for

55

her. As for Joanne, it's anything for a quiet life. She won't quarrel with me but she isn't likely to stand up for me either. Shobna was always the one who was going to find it exciting. Bryony's the unknown quantity.

We don't say a lot on the way to school. Shobna's mum is very quiet. She keeps her eyes on the road and listens to Radio Four. Shobna twitters about something or other from time to time and I give a non-committal grunt. It's not like I'm paying much attention. Shobna's in the front and I'm in the back so I can let it all float by me, the way you do the drone of bees in summer. Some sounds are like that. They pass you by. The real conversation will start when we get to school. I'm staring out of the rain-dimpled windows, watching the headlights cleaving the morning gloom and listening to the beat of the windscreen wipers when Shobna lets out this squeal.

'Annie, look, it's Luke Woodford.'

I see him. In fact, I see them all. It's the whole crew: Luke, Matthew, Anthony, Michael, there next to the sign that proclaims Grovemount as a school specialising in music and the performing arts. If that means the place can turn a drama into a crisis, then that's about right. They're in a huddle at the school gates, talking. Guess who's the main topic of conversation.

'Thanks, Mum,' says Shobna, grabbing her school bag and leading the way.

I know why she's in such a hurry. She wants us to get as close as we can to the boys. Last night was Round One. She can't wait for Round Two. She's in for a disappointment. At our approach the boys look up, but none of them says a word, not even Luke. In spite of the rain running into his eyes, he stares with a brooding intensity. All four watch us pass in studied silence.

'Well,' Shobna says, as intrigued as she is disappointed, 'what do you make of that?'

'I don't make anything of it,' I tell her. 'Any time they want to talk to me about John, I'll be waiting.'

Suddenly Shobna has me down as a cool customer. After a year away and a very public quarrel with Matthew Rice and Luke Woodford, I'm a happening person.

OK, scrub that, a happening person doesn't get stopped in the girls' toilets and called a bitch. I think I said earlier that there isn't a better word than *bitchiness*. Well, there's got to be because, when Naomi Roberts called me a bitch, it was as if I'd been spat on, as if I could feel the word running down my skin, slimy and unpleasant. Bryony knows something's happened the moment I reappear in the corridor.

'Something wrong?' she asks.

'Naomi Roberts just called me an interfering bitch,' I tell her.

'Oh.'

That '*oh*' again, the one that tumbles down a shaft of dismay inside her.

'Something you'd like to tell me?' I ask.

She delivers the vital information in Bryony shorthand: 'Naomi Roberts plus Luke Woodford equals . . . AN ITEM!'

I pull a face. Wonderful. Naomi is only one of the most popular girls in the year.

'I thought it might be something like that.'

A year abroad and I have to learn all the complex geography of relationships that makes Grovemount tick. This I hadn't bargained for. That I'd get grief from the boys, well, I'd expected it. Covering fire from their girlfriends hadn't been part of the equation. I'm still turning this over in my mind when I hear a familiar voice.

'Annie. What a nice surprise. I'd heard you were coming back to us.'

It's Mrs Kruger. She's just locking the LRC – that's library to anybody who doesn't deal in High School acronyms.

'I was wondering if you were going to join the reading club this year. You too, Bryony.'

Even now, knowing she let John down, I hesitate. I'd decided not to go but, meeting Mrs Kruger face to face, I don't like disappointing her. She's always been nice to me.

'Maybe,' I say. 'When's it on?'

Mrs Kruger points to a huge sign on the LRC door and shakes her head.

'Wednesday, 12.30. Doesn't anybody read notices these days?'

I had to give it a miss in Year 9. It clashed with Drama Club and I was Third Urchin in *Oliver Twist*. It occurs to me that, if I had joined, I would have got to know John earlier than I did. I glance at Bryony.

'What do you think?'

Bryony nods. 'I'm in.'

I smile. 'Make that two.'

Mrs Kruger smiles. She is fifty but looks ten, even twenty years younger. She is turning the corner when I remember to be disappointed in her. Nothing is going the way I expected. I had them all lined up, the people who let John down, like a shooting gallery. One by one I would make them face their betrayal. The strangest thing is, they are barely touched by his death.

'She didn't even mention John,' I say.

'Not exactly the first thing you'd talk about, is it?' Bryony says.

I shrug. 'Maybe not, but he was in the LRC every lunchtime. He helped issue the books. You'd think she, of all people, would say something. Nobody even seems to care.'

'It's been four months,' Bryony reminds me. 'Memories fade.'

I feel the tug. John won't let my memories fade.

'That you, Annie?' Mum calls.

She's been off all day. There's a price to pay. It's an early shift tomorrow morning. With work patterns like hers, I don't know how she remembers when to go in.

'It is.'

'Good day?'

Stared at by the boys, called a bitch by Naomi, cold-shouldered in French by her friends (just my luck to be put in with them for conversation), drenched there and back by the drumming rain, why wouldn't it be good?

'You know, the usual.'

Mum sighs. 'I'm sure I talked to my mother when I got home from school.'

'You think?'

'I don't know,' she says. 'Could be you remember the old days the way you'd like them to have been.'

'Could be.'

I pour red grape juice into a glass tumbler. The liquid clucks against the fluted sides.

'Mrs Sorrel rang.'

'Oh.'

It's a big *'Oh,'* heavy with meaning.

'She wants to know if you can babysit this Saturday. I've said Lauren can sleep over.' Mum examines my face. 'You can say no if it makes you uncomfortable.'

I hear the echoes of Mum's quarrel with Dad.

'It does a bit,' I admit.

Then, before I talk myself out of babysitting, and the opportunity to read John's diary again, I add: 'I'll still do it, though. It wouldn't be fair on Lauren and Katie to turn it down.'

I throw in a final comment. 'Besides, I like the money.'

There, naked self interest. That should throw Mum off the scent.

'You're sure you don't mind?' she asks.

I nod. 'I'm sure.'

'Give her a call back then.'

To my dismay, it's Mr Sorrel who answers. That'll make me keep it short and sweet. I never did take to him. He was always so hard on John.

'Hi, Mr Sorrel,' I say, as brightly as I can.

'Oh, Annie, thanks for calling back. Can you help us out?'

'Yes, I'll be there.'

'Great. Usual price.'

'Yes,' I say. 'Usual price.'

'Good girl. I'll pick you and Lauren up about six.'

'See you then.'

The phone goes dead. I find myself staring at the handset. How does he do that? How does he sound so normal after losing his son only four months ago? Even Mrs Sorrel – and she's the one who took it really badly – has started going out again, business functions with her husband, that sort of thing. No way is she over it though. She can pretend as much as she likes. There's still the same shattered look in her eyes. Then there's John's room. She keeps it like a shrine.

'Dad doesn't like me babysitting for the Sorrels, does he?' I ask.

Mum stiffens. 'What makes you say that?'

I don't want to admit to eavesdropping so I resort to one of the old standards: intuition.

'It's a feeling I get.'

The tension slips from Mum's face. 'Well, you're not far wrong. Your dad isn't good with things like this.'

Things like this? I wonder what else is *like this*.

'The Sorrels will drop you back home about half past eleven. Lauren's staying over until Sunday.'

'Mum, you already told me the girls are having a sleep-over. I know the routine.'

'Did I?'

'Yes.'

I'm thinking about Saturday, anticipating the feel of John's diary in my hands. I hope it's Mrs Sorrel driving me home afterwards.

from John's diary
Sunday, 20th April

Today, sitting in the Food Court at Florida Mall, I tried to explain to Annie about the citadel. I thought it would make me seem strong. I would be somebody who could take it all on the chin. I'd be the Spartan boy hiding the fox in his shirt and allowing it to eat his entrails before he'll admit to concealing it. Somehow, it didn't work out the way I expected. She looked around nervously but the others were too busy with their own conversation to be listening to us.

'It's what keeps them out,' I said.

I started to pick up signs. Her eyes flicked away from me. Was I making her uncomfortable?

'Out? Out of what?'

'Out of the heart of me, of course. The citadel has many walls, rings of defence that I can throw up against them.'

Annie frowned. Did she think I was making it up? Was that it? I took a second stab at explaining myself. If there was one person in the whole world I hoped would understand, it was Annie.

'Please, Annie,' I begged. 'Please understand!'

I'm not sure she did. She couldn't hide her discomfort.

'I let them think they've won,' I tell her. 'It's either that, or get hurt even worse. I just want them off my back. Sometimes I plead and beg. It's all an act. They don't know what it takes to break me. So long as they don't get inside the citadel, I can carry on. I'll pass all my exams. I'll get away from them and make a life for myself. You see. I'm the one who's going to have the last laugh.'

I looked at her, willing her to understand, and told her my little dream: 'I imagine a school reunion twenty years from now. They're in dead-end jobs. That's all a bunch of cretins like that deserve. I walk in the room and there they are, a bunch of grey, disappointed

61

men. In contrast, I'm rich, fulfilled. While they've run to fat, I've got my life together. I'm paying a personal trainer. I eat all the right stuff.'

Annie broke eye contact. Maybe it was too soon to talk to her like this. She'll think I'm obsessive. I know how people think. Jeez, that's how it is with Stress Hound, my own father, he thinks I'm a complete ding-a-ling.

'You don't get it, do you?' I said, aching for her to understand

'Of course I do,' she answered. 'But how can it go on like this? Doesn't anybody ever try to help you? Haven't you told anyone what you're going through?'

The way she said it, she didn't really understand at all. Annie still thinks this is about telling somebody, seeking help, getting the teachers to stop the bullying. I've tried that. I went to Mum. Nothing changed. People helping you, that's what happens in the world of hope. I don't live there any more. I'm beyond that. Survival, that's the name of the game. In this life, in this town, I don't expect anything. Being happy, taking control of my life, that's all in the future. But Annie couldn't come to terms with that. Try as I might to explain the strategies I use to survive, she just couldn't get her head round it. She wants there to be a Seventh Cavalry, a bunch of good guys who'll come riding over the horizon and make things all right. Well, tough. I stopped believing in that stuff a long time ago.

Everybody has a breaking point, that's what I was trying to tell her. Find it and you can crush even the strongest spirit. Nobody understands that better than George Orwell in *1984*. When they put the rat in the cage Winston Smith begs them to take Julia, his lover, not him. That's how they storm the citadel. They've cracked the code, crushed the one thing he cares about. They've destroyed love. Now there is nothing left to defend. That's what Rice and Woodford will never understand. They can cause me physical pain, they can make me look ridiculous, they can even make me beg. But that's not the rat, that's not it at all. There are still places inside myself where I can go where I am safe. The rat doesn't get in.

'Oh, I've told people,' I say, wondering how she can keep on asking the same questions, over and over.

Doesn't she realise I've tried everything?

'Mr Storey even arranged a little conference in his office.'

I can still remember the day. Mr Storey, ever the head teacher, sat there with this self-satisfied look on his face. The buck stops with me, it seemed to say. I'll soon sort this out. He kept asking me if I was satisfied with what he'd done, all part of the school's No-Blame Bullying Policy. No blame! Now isn't that an interesting idea? What's wrong with the dipstick? This isn't about him; it's about me. He isn't the one getting picked on, I am. I don't know what he expected. Did he think I would shake hands with Woodford and Rice, is that it? There you go, no blame. Well, he can stick his no blame. Does he really think we're all equal, the kid who's lying on the ground and the one who jumped on his head? That we're as bad as each other?

Here's the unadorned truth: I'm not to blame, those scum are. I'm a bit overweight. That doesn't mean they can break my tooth the way they did. I prefer reading to wiring myself up to an MP3. That doesn't mean they can smear my face with make-up. I don't want a civilised discussion. I want protection. Did Storey think I would forgive them and walk off into the sunset to the sound of swelling strings? Forget it. Nothing old Storey did was going to make any difference. So I shut him out. It was all an act, of course, me being strong, sticking up for myself, not needing another person in the whole world. But it's not how I really feel. I just feel alone. The other boys said they'd stop, of course. They did what any bully would do. They admitted the small stuff: the teasing, the flicking, the following round. The big stuff they denied. Mum acted like she was actually grateful for what Mr Storey had done.

But why couldn't she go all the way and make it stop? Doesn't she understand nothing's changed? No matter how I acted in front of Storey, I can't do this myself. Why couldn't she fight my corner to the bitter end? That's right, Mum: yell, scream, do anything, so long as you stop them destroying me.

Back home she sensed I was unhappy. Even then, she hardly said a word. She went about her business as usual, as if there was nothing more to be said. What more did I want? I don't know, maybe I just needed her to hold me, tell me it wasn't my fault, tell me I wasn't bringing it all on myself by being some kind of pathetic weirdo. Maybe I wanted her to sit me down and ask why I still wasn't happy. Maybe I needed a mother, easy as that. But, as usual, she wasn't there for me. Much as I love her, with every day that passes she seems to fade further from me. The way I see it, one day she won't be there at all.

Anyway, Annie just kept on asking her questions. Didn't Mrs Kruger help? What about Ms, not Miss, Leather? Weren't they on your side? Didn't either of them help? Well, sorry to disillusion you, Annie, but nobody helps the fat kid – and I mean nobody. He walks alone.

Suddenly Annie, even kind, understanding Annie, was like the others. Why am I such an outcast? Why can't I reach them? Why was she banging on about what other people could do? Didn't she understand? Nobody's going to call off the pack. All the stuff at school, it wasn't about what they could do at all, it was about me and how I could survive. As I write this I'm starting to understand that it's going to be like this until I get away from them. My time with Annie is only an interlude. Nobody understands, not really. Nobody who lives in the normal world ever will. Two more years, that's all it will take. I have to pray the citadel will hold that long. Then life can start for real.

Annie

Saturday, 13th September

On the way to the Sorrels' house Lauren and Katie want to sit in the back. That means I have to sit in the front next to Mr Sorrel. He feels the pressure to make small talk.

'How's school?'

What do I say, that a watered-down version of what happened to his son is starting to happen to me? Just because I'm not isolated like John, alone like John, ripped up like John, doesn't mean it hasn't been a tough week. Suddenly I understand what it's like to spend your life walking on glass. Still, what did I expect? When it all came to a head at the Mega-Bowl last Sunday night some part of me really did think the worst was over. I would square up to the rest of the world and the rest of the world would blink first.

I'm starting to realise how dumb I was to think that way. My big bust-up with Luke didn't change anything. All this week has been is a big, fat nothing. For a start, the Gang of Four don't even seem interested in me. Matthew looks away every time we come within ten metres of one another. He seems genuinely embarrassed. Same with Anthony and Michael really, but since when did they matter? Even Luke feigns lack of interest. He's content to let his pet Rottweiler, Naomi, do the talking. And can she talk! There's me thinking at last, more by luck than anything else, I'd got the boys to take me seriously and all I've done is make an enemy of Naomi. If you want to understand what that means, imagine concentrated vinegar forced through a tube under 100 tonnes of pressure, and the whole stinging jet of the stuff aimed straight at me. What was meant to be a grand settling of scores is descending into a squalid mess. Wonderful!

I bet you're really proud of me, John.

'Annie?'

It's Mr Sorrel's voice. What did he ask me? Oh yes, how's school?

'You know,' I mumble, 'OK.' Well, once you get over the piranha bites, the sting of vinegar and the non-stop feeling you're letting down one of the nicest, gentlest people you ever met in your life.

'You're doing well, I hear, on schedule for some good O level results.'

Let's just stick to the basics, Annie girl, the stuff you can tell this guy. 'They call them GCSEs now,' I tell him.

'Of course,' he says. 'I knew that. So you're doing well?'

'I'm in the top set for everything, yes. I should get mostly As.'

My answers come out this side of frosty. He must have noticed. I'm being a bit less than subtle. Not that it makes any difference. He keeps going.

'What's your favourite subject?'

Oh, give me a break. What is this, Platitudes, a game for all the family? 'I like the Arts, Humanities. English is my real love, literature. That's what I want to do at university, that and maybe Drama.'

Mr Sorrel blinks rapidly and a dry croak enters his voice. It's not like him to look flustered. 'John always liked English.'

Just before he said that, I noticed him glance in the rear-view mirror. He didn't want Katie to hear. At the mention of John's name, I feel a tremor of surprise. Mr Sorrel barely seems to care most of the time. Then, out of the blue, he brings it up himself. Have I misjudged him?

'I remember.'

'Yes, of course you do,' says Mr Sorrel. 'He wrote poetry, you know.'

I know. He showed them to me in Florida. I don't let on, of course, same as I don't let on I've been in John's room. Mrs Sorrel keeps his bedroom like a shrine. Everything is the same way it was the day he did it, right down to his school uniform lying draped over his chair. Officially, Mum's the only member of our family to have seen John's room. Imagine what would happen if they knew what I was doing on babysitting nights.

'He did mention it,' I say. That's it, short and sweet. Don't try to be clever. Don't give anything away.

'Did you read any of them, his poems?'

Yes, of course I did. Portrait of the Artist as a Tortured Adolescent, that's what popped into my mind as I was reading them. Listen to me, I sound really cruel. It isn't my idea of poetry though, all this shredding your heart in public. Same with the diary. I mean, why do people keep diaries anyway? They can't be writing for themselves. They're writing for an eavesdropper, aren't they? That, or if they're really full of themselves, maybe they're writing for posterity, some future audience desperate for their innermost thoughts. Didn't John tell me once that he wanted to write the Great British Novel?

For the second time in five minutes I realise Mr Sorrel is waiting for an answer from me. What was his latest penetrating question? Oh yes, poetry.

'No, he never showed them to me,' I lie. 'Too personal, I suppose.'

'Yes, probably. Denise has read them. They made her really upset.'

The noise level drops in the back. We've got an audience. Mr Sorrel is suddenly self-conscious and we complete the journey in silence. I've never been so grateful for two pairs of inquisitive eight-year-old ears. I don't think Mr Sorrel was much of a father when his son was alive. What makes him want to start now John is dead? Entering the Sorrels' house I feel the same sensation I've experienced twice before, same as when you walk in a church when you're not sure you believe it all anymore. I'm trespassing, spying on John. But he wants me to spy.

'Hello, Annie love,' says Mrs Sorrel.

She's wearing a black dress, that's it, the classic little black dress. Come to think of it, the three times I've seen her since America all she's worn is black. I wonder for a moment if it's fashion, or mourning.

'Hi, Mrs Sorrel.'

'It's good of you to do this for us.'

'You are paying me, remember.'

She smiles. 'Of course we are.'

'How long do I give the girls?'

What I mean is, when can I get my hands on John's diary? When do I get to walk back in his mind?

'Tell them to go up to their room at half past nine. They can watch TV, or play games until half past ten, then it's lights out and not another murmur. We'll be back at half past eleven.'

An hour to read John's diary, a bit less if they push the boundaries. I might even finish it this time.

'There's plenty of food in the fridge. Just help yourself.'

Mr Sorrel is hovering round the front door, slipping his jacket on. 'Are you ready, Denise? Annie knows her way round.'

You got that right, Mr Sorrel. I picture John's diary in the top drawer of his desk. Yes, I know my way round.

The whole evening I'm on tenterhooks. It takes every ounce of patience I can muster not to snap at Lauren and Katie. Honestly, how irritating can two kids be? They're in and out of the living room by the minute and all I want to do is sit and brood. When I do get the time to think it's mostly about John. I also think about school. Ms Leather – sorry, Mrs Linklater – took me to one side today. I think she's got a whiff of what's going on with Naomi.

'Is something the matter?' she asked.

I shrugged. When you get right down to it, what's the matter is the way everyone like her should have protected John and didn't. I so want to be in Mrs Linklater's good books, but didn't she fail John like everyone else? She winds up saying something like:

'Well, if you want to talk, you know where I am.'

The question is, where was she when John needed her?

Lauren and Katie don't make it easy for me. I'm counting the minutes until I can read John's diary, but will they settle down? For goodness' sake, who'd be a parent? It's a quarter to eleven before they start to calm down, almost eleven o'clock before I feel safe to slip into John's room. I glance at the posters on the wall. One I recognised the first time I baby-sat. It's Kurt Cobain. The significance of the Nirvana lead singer didn't escape me, of course. I already knew John's weird taste in music. But there was something else, something so glaringly obvious the Sorrels must have known. Cobain killed himself. I was a bit shocked they hadn't taken the poster down after what happened. Didn't they realise?

It gets worse though. The second poster I didn't recognise. I had to do a bit of research on the Internet. Eventually I found him. The guy in the poster is Ian Curtis, lead singer of a Manchester band from the eighties called Joy Division. Guess what? Got it in one. He took his life when he was suffering from depression. Another rock'n'roll suicide.

As soon as I found out about him I had this question scratching away at me: when did John put this stuff up? Did it mean he'd been thinking about killing himself for a while? If the posters had been up for some time, then yes, that could be it. But if they were a recent addition, was it a warning? Or am I reading too much into a couple of posters? Maybe he just liked a bit of electronic depression. There are plenty of kids who dress in black, go gothic and wallow in designer misery and they don't top themselves.

To be honest, what I know about psychology wouldn't fill a picture postcard. I've never been through the kind of downer John must have suffered, not ever. Could the posters just be a statement, standard teenage angst? I've heard that there are lame-brained journos coining phrases like rock'n'roll suicide, as though it's a fun thing to do. Sure, like it's cool or something to mess with those kinds of ideas. The way I see it, play with Death and you're going to lose – big time. One thing's for certain, there's no way I can ask Mr and Mrs Sorrel. That would mean admitting I've been in John's room.

Looking away from the posters I listen for a few moments before sliding open John's drawer. There's the diary. You're not going to believe this, but the first time I read it I actually wiped it clean after. Yes, as if the Sorrels were going to fingerprint it, or do DNA swabs! I've watched way too much TV. I'm so paranoid I always put it back exactly as I find it too. It's my worst nightmare, the thought of Mr Sorrel confronting me, asking who the hell I think I am, sticking my nose where it doesn't belong. Then there's the thought of Mrs Sorrel's face, the disappointment in those sad eyes, and that's worse.

I hear footsteps on the landing and tense. Edging to the door I listen. Bare feet pad along the carpet to the bathroom. I use the dimmer switch to extinguish the light. After that I wait for thirty seconds, maybe a minute, in the dark. Don't go downstairs, I beg. Don't for God's sake call my name. My heart stutters when I hear the toilet flush. The footsteps return to the girls' room and the door clicks shut. Slowly I release the breath I've been holding.

It's a moment or two before I feel safe to turn the dimmer switch back up and open the diary. It isn't printed or anything. There are no dates or calendars. It's an unlined notebook, good quality. Black and shiny. The word *Circa* is embossed on the back. The paper is crisp and cream. It's obviously expensive, a present maybe. John wrote with a Mont Blanc pen on cream paper, always in the same colour. The pen is still in the drawer. I look at the handwriting. It's small, neat. The punctuation is meticulous, right down to the use of semi-colons, the ones nobody in my class can understand (and I think that includes our teacher). There is hardly a single crossing out anywhere. John was serious about his diary.

I read the holiday entries again. OK, it takes up precious time, but I want to see them again, the entries about me. It bothers me that he fancied Bryony before me, but that's stupid. I didn't even want him to fancy me, so what's to be jealous about? Eventually I come to the page that made me frown the first time I turned it.

Something said in an unguarded moment. He let it slip. The old get let it slip. Is there really some secret? What does he mean? He can't be telling the truth. He just can't. But why say it?

That's all there is. But what's this entry about? What did Mr Sorrel say? What was the secret? I read on for about twelve pages last time and there's only one other mention of it. After that, everything seems to get back to normal, at least as normal as John's life ever was. I turn the page to Wednesday, 23rd April. It's all about the day we went to Universal Studios. John hung around outside the Incredible Hulk and Duelling Dragons waiting for the rest of us. It didn't matter what anybody said. Nothing was going to coax him onto the rollercoasters. He made excuses. It would make him sick. He didn't like going upside down. We all knew what it was really. It was fear, pure and simple. But what's wrong with that? John knew his limitations.

I'm three quarters of the way through the book when I hear a key scrape in the lock downstairs. The Sorrels! I glance at my watch. It's eleven-twenty. What's wrong with them? Who ever heard of hiring a babysitter and getting home early? I slide the diary back in the drawer, checking it's positioned perfectly in the centre. That done, I slip my shoes back on and go to the door. Please don't be on your way up the stairs, I beg inwardly. Please don't be waiting for me. Breath shuddering through my chest, I turn the door handle. I imagine Mr Sorrel on the top stair, gazing at me in disbelief. Sucking in a final gulp of air, I slip out. There's nobody on the landing, nobody on the stairs.

'Annie?'

It's Mrs Sorrel. She is speaking quietly so as not to wake the girls. I arrive at the top of the stairs just as she reaches the bottom.

'I was checking on the girls,' I tell her.

That was a mistake. Isn't it only people with something to hide that volunteer unnecessary information?

'You really are conscientious, aren't you?' Mrs Sorrel says.

Mr Sorrel appears. Is that suspicion in his eyes? Why do I have to blurt things out like that?

'Oh, I just wanted to make sure they'd gone off to sleep,' I answer.

There you go, Annie, you're doing it again. Idiot, idiot. What if old Sorrel has rumbled me? What if he interrogates me on the way home? That's when Mrs Sorrel says the words I've been longing to hear: 'Phil can't drive,' she says, as if sharing a secret. 'He's had a few too many. I'll run you home.'

Right, that explains the glassy stare. Stress Hound is drunk.

'Oh,' I say, trying to hide the relief in my voice. 'I'll get my coat.'

I brush against Mr Sorrel. I can feel his eyes on me. Does he suspect? By the time I'm halfway down the front path I've dismissed the idea. Why would he? Annie, get a life.

from John's diary
Thursday, 24th April

Today I flew. We drove down to the northern Everglades, both families. The designer eight-year-olds got their designer photos taken with a designer baby alligator. Its jaws were secured with designer tape. Don't want any designer bites on our designer skin, do we, girls? OK, that's enough with the designer joke. Why do I always have to overdo things? We ate in a restaurant that served alligator steaks. I didn't have one but Dad did, of course. He'd eat roast cockroaches with a side order of razor blades if it gave him any kudos. He's just got to show what a big man he is.

Hang on, I don't know why I'm doing this. Why lash out at Dad when he's been on his best behaviour? You know what, he went a whole day today without a single nasty comment. He didn't put me down once. There was no sarcasm, no cruelty. He was my dad. He challenged us all to a race. Annie and I were way out in front. I've got a feeling he let us win. The whole day, we were a family. I like that word, family. Maybe that's all I've ever wanted, to be part of a proper family. It felt relaxed, a day without a cloud. Why can't it always be this way?

We went on an air-boat ride looking at alligators and turtles. We crept up to this clump of reeds and there it was, a nest full of baby alligators. We watched marsh birds rise into the sky. But the highlight of the day was when I flew. OK, maybe I'm stretching it a bit to say I flew. What I did was go para-sailing. Let's say that again. John Sorrel, former wimp, actually got strapped into a parachute and floated four hundred feet up from the back of a speedboat. Dad went first, then Rob, then Annie. All the while I was being strapped into the harness my heart was slamming in my rib cage. But when it came right down to it, it was fantastic. I just started to lift. No big jerk, no sudden tug, effortlessly I rose into the sky. I won't say I wasn't scared to start with. It took a couple of minutes before I stopped clinging to the straps of the harness. Then, far below, I could see everybody waving at me. Forcing my heart back down my throat, I waved back.

Then I really was flying. I was so free. Weightless, almost thoughtless, for maybe the first time in my life nothing was preying on my mind. All there was was me and the azure sky, me and the spring breeze, me and the rush of the lake below. Yes, all there was was me and the big, wide, beautiful world. Even when the guys in charge of the boat started goofing about, shaking the rope, I didn't panic. I waved and let myself bounce and sway. Then, when they started to reel me in, it wasn't relief I felt but disappointment. There was still one surprise to come, however. Just as I was expecting to step onto the boat I heard one of them calling: 'Do you want to get wet, buddy?'

So I shouted: 'Yes, time to dunk me.'

Next thing I was splashing into the lake up to my waist. I didn't squeal or sulk. I went with the flow. I did wonder if they had giant snapping turtles lurking in there but I didn't cop out. Then, finally, they hauled me back on board. I could hardly believe it. I'd been a good sport. I caught Dad's eye. He actually looked halfway impressed. He even patted me on the back when I sat down.

As I sit here writing, I find myself wondering about what he said the other day. Was it just something said in anger, the big, fat secret he waved in front of my face? I might phone our Jessica when I get home. She'll know. God, I hope he was making it up. I hope there is no secret. There can't be. I hope it's not Mum. Not Mum. I couldn't take another day without her. She's the one who holds me together. I know she lets me down, but there's never any doubt about one thing: she cares. Even after a good day like today I can never feel the same about Dad. I'm always tense when he's around, wondering when he's going to blow. Mum's different. Soon as we're alone, I can relax. The moment she's out of his shadow, life goes back to being the way it should be. If anything ever changed that, I don't know what I'd do. I need her to be there for me. I can't lose her. I can't.

*

Three more days, two really, that's all there is left. Then Annie goes back to Departure Bay and I go back to Hell. At least I'll be able to survive. I'll have Annie. I don't just mean her memory either. We're going to keep in touch. Suddenly I feel so strong. Today I learned to fly. Today I learned to look down on the world and see it for what it is. There are a million ways of being, a million fresh starts, a million opportunities. Grovemount isn't the beginning and end of things. It's just a lousy little interlude. One day, not so distant, I will leave it all behind. Then another day, just over the horizon, I will look back and wonder why it ever seemed important, why I ever let it hurt me. All I've got to do is live for that new day dawning. Annie gives me the strength to do that.

Tomorrow

Through skeins of English rain,
through a lattice-work
of memories,
through the rainbow light
of the mind's prism,
another day beckons.

Through a thousand morning mists,
through dreams unborn
and joys unforeseen,
through the scent of a loved one's hair,
another
better
day beckons.

Annie

Sunday, 14th September

Did I lead him on?

It was one afternoon, a couple of days before the end of the holiday. We'd just arrived back at our villa from Busch Gardens. 'We' is our family and the Sorrels. Sometimes it felt as if the eight of us were becoming attached at the hip. I don't think Mum and Dad were too keen on the arrangement but they went along with it for Lauren's sake. Even after their day out, Katie and Lauren still wanted to go to Old Town to use the trampolines. Again! Most evenings, even after a hard day Disney-ing, they would beg and plead until we took a detour to the place. I ask you, how many somersaults can you do in one holiday?

Anyway, I said I was bored with Old Town and couldn't I stay in the villa? Right away, John said the same. It would be no big deal to pick him up on the way back. I knew what he was thinking. My neck burned at the thought of it. It was obvious how he felt about me. Why couldn't Mum and Dad see it? Or did they just think it was harmless, kid's stuff? I know they still thought of me as their little girl. The point is, this wasn't good. I liked being with John but I just didn't fancy him. There was a lot of umming and ahing from our parents, and once or twice, seeing John staring at me the way he did, I very nearly agreed to go to Old Town after all. But in the end there didn't seem an easy way to change my mind and the cars pulled out of the driveway without us.

'I'm going for a swim,' I said.

John smiled as if I had read some thought in the back of his mind. 'I'll join you.'

It wasn't what I wanted to hear. A voice in my head was screaming: how the hell do I get out of this? Letting John down gently was like trying to hold a soap bubble in your hand. No matter how much you tried, its fragility was going to tell in the end. Not knowing quite what to say or do, I slid into the pool, taking great care not to meet his eyes. Every atom of my being became a piece of elastic pulled to breaking point. I heard the splash as he slipped into the water behind me. Kicking against the side I ploughed up and down the pool. It was hard to avoid John. These villa pools are tiny, little more than an extended bath really. The space became a noose, tightening, tightening.

'I think I'll get out now,' I said.

He gave me the puppy eyes. 'Not yet,' he said. 'You must know how I feel, Annie.'

A plug of intense, peppery embarrassment formed in my throat. 'I know.'

Why, oh why, didn't I go to Old Town? What was another trudge round the gift shops compared to this?

'What about you, how do you feel about me?'

Don't do this to yourself, I thought.

'I like you.'

'Just like?'

He had moved in front of me. I was aware of a large insect, like a mantis, splayed on the netting round the pool.

'John . . .'

That's when he touched me. His fingertips rested on my cheek a moment, then traced a line down to my lips. I wanted to stop him but I didn't. Why? That's what I keep asking myself.

'Don't speak,' he said.

His fingers touched my throat. I could barely breathe. Then, without removing his hand, he leaned forward.

'Annie,' he said.

His voice was husky. At last his fingers moved away. The terrible constriction in my throat started to relax, but only for a moment. Soon the fingers were touching my chin, my cheeks. He leaned into me and we kissed, or rather I yielded to his kiss.

78

'Annie,' he said again, pulling back for a moment. Then, agonisingly, he repeated my name: 'My Annie.'

That's what did it. Those two words, they broke the spell. My palms flew to his chest and I pushed him away.

'Don't,' I said. 'John, this isn't right.'

'Too soon, you mean?'

John, I thought, with you it will always be too soon. But, did I say that?

'Yes,' I answered feebly. 'Too soon.'

We were still standing that way, his hands still cupping my face, his breath still feathering my lips, when the beam of a car's headlights swung over the pool.

'They're back!' I gasped. In an instant John was threshing his way up and down the pool in a clumsy, frantic attempt at the crawl. What was he doing?

'Annie?' It was Mum.

'Out at the pool,' I called.

She appeared at the poolside. Seeing John splashing like a demented walrus, his idea of an alibi, I think (we weren't up to anything, honest!), she burst out laughing.

'Slow down, John,' she said. 'You're going to empty all the water out.'

He stopped and stood blinking at her, a toddler who's been caught with his fingers in the sweetie jar.

'What's this, trying to keep fit?'

'Yes,' he said. 'Working off the blubber.'

'How come you're back?' I asked.

'The mobile,' Mum said. 'I forgot it. We got up to the 192 and realised you wouldn't have any way of contacting us if there was an emergency.'

Emergency? Oh, there was an emergency all right, but not the way she meant.

'You haven't seen it hanging around, have you?'

Odd phrase that. How does a phone hang around? It's not like a bat. Anyway, meeting John's eyes for the briefest, most tortured second, I flew out of the pool and wrapped myself in a towel.

'I'll help you look,' I said.

'You're not coming in here dripping over the carpet,' Mum said.

So I stood towelling myself dry, achingly aware of John's eyes on me.

'There,' I said. 'Bone dry.'

'I can't find this damned phone,' Mum said, turning the cushions over.

'Tell you what, Mum,' I said, seizing the chance. 'Give me five minutes and I'll come with you after all. Saves worrying about phones.'

Mum was standing, hands on hips, scanning the living room. 'You're sure?'

'It makes sense.'

Mum nodded. 'What about you, John?' she said.

There was disappointment in his look as he turned to face me. 'Give me five minutes, Mrs Chapman,' he said, gathering his clothes from the sun-lounger and vanishing into the bathroom.

As I got dressed I could still hear Mum puzzling over the whereabouts of the phone.

'Beats me what happened to it,' she said.

'Yes,' I said. 'Me too.'

I'm not sure I sounded too convincing. I'd found the mobile straight away, thirty seconds after I climbed out of the pool. Glancing in the direction of the door, I'd slipped it out of sight. My escape route.

from John's diary
Friday, 25th April

We fly back tomorrow. The dream is almost over. Will it be enough to keep me going when I get back to Grovemount, or will things go back to the way they were? I know that on the flight home I will struggle to re-create the sensation, struggle and fail. Life is cruel. How can it end like this? How can I let Annie go home to Departure Bay? How can we just walk away from each other as if nothing has happened? None of it makes any sense.

Yesterday we kissed. I could hardly believe it was happening, me falling in love for the first time, and being loved in return. It was so beautiful. I followed her into the pool and ran my fingers through the droplets of water on her throat. I traced a path down her skin. She does feel the way I do. She does. I've had my doubts. So many times I've thought I was reading her wrong and I started to shrivel inside. Now I know better. She is my Annie, mine. I've found somebody who cares, really cares, about me. All the while I held her my heart was pounding in my chest.

It's hard to believe how much things have changed. Life at home is still the same. I muddle through, bouncing between Stress Hound and Agony Kitten like a ping pong ball. But there's something to look forward to. There's Annie.

Annie

Monday, 15th September

It's Drama, one of Ms Leather's classes. No, I've done it again, forgotten about her bizarre Beauty and the Beast hook-up with the Missing Link. Make that *Mrs Linklater's* class. It really doesn't get any easier to call her that. Still, we're doing *Macbeth*. The theme today is vaunting ambition. It's a good word that, vaunting. I like it. The idea is to come up with a contemporary interpretation of the play. Our setting is a tough estate in an unnamed city. Macbeth is an up and coming petty crook and street fighter – Mac – who wants to take over the gang. Ms Leather has had us in two lines advancing on each other, clicking fingers, acting provocatively. We all enjoyed that. There's a stylised fight. No contact, you understand, no matter how hard some of the lads try to bend the rules. You can guess how it turns out. On the way back from the fight Macbeth and Banquo come across three old crones staggering out of a boozer, the worse for wear with drink.

'It's Mac,' says one. 'Toughest young buck on the whole estate.'

'Estate nothing,' says the second. 'He's got it in him to control the whole West Side.'

'You're both of you wrong,' says the last. 'One day he'll have this whole city in the palm of his hand.'

This is typical of Mrs Linklater. She's always looking to make things relevant. We do a lot of solo stuff. I'm enjoying myself. Drama has always been one of my best subjects. Plus, Naomi isn't in my set for Drama, so that's one spitting viper out of my hair. Also, out of the Gang of Four there's only Matthew, and so far I have managed to steer well clear of him.

'OK,' says Mrs Linklater. 'Let's look at one particular scene.

82

This is when Lady Macbeth encourages her husband to assassinate the King. How are we going to do this?'

Bryony's hand shoots up first. I think she fancies being Lady Macbeth.

'Bryony?'

'Macbeth's girlfriend is winding him up to challenge for leadership of the gang. How's about, instead of sneaking up to the bed chamber to do the kill, we have a knife fight? It's more exciting.'

There's agreement all round, especially from the lads.

'We can't call the girlfriend Lady something though. It doesn't fit.'

'What then?' Mrs Linklater asks.

'Just use our own names,' Bryony suggests.

She wants the part all right.

'Very good,' says Mrs Linklater. 'Well, you've done your bit, Bryony. Let's get somebody else to do the hard work.'

I glance at Bryony. Crestfallen isn't the word for the look on her face. She really wanted the part.

'Annie.'

I look around self-consciously.

'Yes you,' says Mrs Linklater, laughing. 'You did really well in the warm-ups. You're a born actress.'

She's got that right. Give me a stage and I take it over. Everybody says so. This time, however, there's the faintest tingle down my spine. It's only a one in thirteen chance, but what if . . .?

'Right, we've got our Lady Macbeth. Now for Macbeth himself.'

Not Matthew, anybody but Matthew. But it's one in thirteen. They're good odds.

'Come on, Matthew,' Mrs Linklater says. 'Let's see what you're made of.'

Thirteen to one. Good odds, but not good enough. Seeing him making his way forward, I want to dissolve and trickle away through the floor. As Matthew steps away from the line there is a low murmur. My gaze travels around the class. Do they know what happened at the Mega-Bowl? I give Mrs Linklater a look of dumb despair. How can you do this to me? Is a woman as intelligent as you really that oblivious to what's going on in this school?

Within minutes I'm standing behind and above Matthew. He's sitting on a chair and I'm the vile seductress, using my feminine wiles to get him to challenge for leadership of the Gang. I don't feel like a seductress. The last thing I want to do is touch Matthew. But that's exactly what Mrs Linklater has in mind.

'OK, people,' she says. 'How's Annie going to get her way?'

There are plenty of suggestions, some of them a bit crude for Mrs Linklater's liking.

'Don't go over the top,' she says. 'Now, Annie, I think the general view is right. Get in closer. Be more physical.'

From where I'm standing I can't see Matthew's face, but I can sense his discomfort. It oozes from him. Equally uneasy, I put my hands on his shoulders and lean in. My cheek brushes his and I find myself speaking: 'You can take him, Mac. You know you can. Look in your heart. You want to be the Big Man, you know you do. Do it, Mac.'

So far it's acting.

'You'll find me grateful, Mac, if you know what I mean.'

That sets off a few giggles and the odd *Whooo*. Then I'm not acting.

'You know how to kill. You've done it before.'

Then I'm aware of two things. There's Mrs Linklater, seemingly unaware of the tension between Matthew and me, praising my performance, saying something about a bit of poetic licence. What I said about killing, it wasn't licence, it was the truth. The words are barely out of my mouth when I see Matthew staring up at me, eyes hard, whispering: 'Why are you doing this?'

I spin on my heel and walk away, leaving him to gaze after me.

I'm about to follow Bryony out of the Drama Hall when Matthew catches up with me.

'We need to talk,' he says.

'I don't think so.'

84

But he tries again. 'You've got me all wrong.'

'Is that right?'

I'm aware of Bryony watching from the doorway. Mrs Linklater's got to be around somewhere too.

'You think I'm some kind of monster,' he says.

I'm quick with my interruption. 'You said it, Matthew.'

'What the hell do you think I've done?'

'You made John's life a misery. Say you didn't.'

Matthew's holding his arms out, palms upturned. 'We took a rise out of him. It happens all the time.'

'A rise?' I cry. 'Is that what you call it? Tell me about the make-up, Matthew. Tell me about the bra incident. Go on, make light of that. What kind of twisted mind thinks up something like that? Abuse is what that is. You were torturing another human being.'

Matthew looks as if I've slapped his face. 'I told Luke he was going a bit far.'

'Big of you,' I sneer.

'We've played tricks on other kids,' Matthew says. He sounds really pathetic.

'This wasn't other kids,' I seethe. 'This was John. You knew he hated what you were doing. Didn't you ever ask yourself what effect it was having? What if he couldn't take it?'

'Annie, honest to God,' Matthew says, sounding so defensive, 'he never said anything. Surely if he didn't like it . . .'

I've had enough. Walking away, I flash a comment: 'And if he had said something, are you really saying you'd have stopped?'

The door is swinging shut when I hear Matthew's voice. 'If I'd known, Annie. If he'd just said something.'

from John's diary
Sunday, 27th April

I'm back.

As we drove through the dawn light from the airport it didn't feel like a homecoming. The only thing that really mattered I was leaving behind me. The weather suited my mood. Cataracts of mist clung to the windows of the taxi. Fine raindrops drifted across the fields. The whole world seemed to be crying.

This afternoon Stress Hound watched the football. We went to a couple of matches when I was younger but, when I wasn't interested, he took it as a sign that I was a hopeless wimp. Mum was on the phone to our Jessica, telling her about the holiday. I wish I was the oldest kid, not the middle one. It must be great to be Jessica. She's done it. She's escaped the nest and she's building a life for herself. Two more years, that's all, then I can be off, too. Katie was on her mobile telling her friends about the holiday. She slipped into this weird transatlantic accent. All you could hear was: 'Like, I'm in Disney and there's Lauren Chapman. I mean, what are the chances?'

What were the chances? To meet Annie, to fall in love, then to lose her, all in the space of two short weeks. Every day was so good. I was alive. But now I'm back and nothing matters any more.

The pack will be waiting. For two weeks I've had the pressure of Dad, but that's nothing to the pressure of the Gang of Four. They'll be sharpening their little knives already. They'll never give up. They'll never stop. So I've got to endure. That's my fate, to survive two more years. Then I can get away to university and life can start for real.

Annie
I saw you
on a bright, hot day
Far from home.
You were as shy as I was,
Hesitant as me.
They pushed you forward
To make small talk.
But small words
Grow bigger.
They swell
And occupy spaces inside you.
They fill hearts.
You,
Thousands of miles from here,
Fill mine.

part two

The two diaries of John Sorrow

Annie

'Annie.'

It's Mrs Linklater, reeling me in. I exchange glances with Bryony. This was inevitable, I suppose. I knew Mrs Linklater was around somewhere during my confrontation with Matthew. I've been hoping I got away with it but it looks like she overheard us after all. Curiosity leaps in Bryony's eyes.

'I've got Spanish,' I tell her.

I say it more in hope than expectation. I've got a feeling she isn't going to let this one go.

'You'll be there in a moment. I'll give you a late pass for Ms Hernandez.'

A sigh escapes me. For the second time I meet Bryony's eyes. 'I'll catch up with you,' I tell her.

Bryony glances in Mrs Linklater's direction, registers the possibility of deep interrogation and nods.

'You and Matthew,' Mrs Linklater says, once Bryony is safely out of the door. 'Would you like to tell me about it?'

I let my voice go flat. 'There's nothing to tell.'

'Even from inside the stock cupboard I could tell that wasn't true. What were the raised voices about, Annie?'

Up to this point I've been keeping my gaze averted. At those words I look her square in the eye. The worm has turned. 'You really don't know?'

'Does this have something to do with what happened to John Sorrel?'

My voice rises an octave. 'Of course it does!'

Mrs Linklater frowns. 'I wasn't aware you two were friends.'

I'm confused. Surely she's got to know more than she's letting on.

'Not here, no, we weren't. We met on holiday.'

A furrowed brow tells me I'm not getting through. 'But you've been in Canada,' Mrs Linklater says.

I explain, stumbling over the details of my story in my hurry to get it out. How can she not know?

'And you blame Matthew?'

'Don't you? The police interviewed him. They interviewed all of them.'

'All?'

'Anthony, Michael.' I grimace, remembering the swollen veins in Luke's temple, the fixed hostility of his stare. 'Luke.'

Mrs Linklater gives a dismissive shake of her head. 'Annie, the police interviewed dozens of pupils.'

I want to scream. I want to shake her. What's wrong with her? Doesn't she get it? Is she that ignorant of the life of this school? Doesn't she know what they did?

'But they killed him! John told me.'

That look again. She's unresponsive, almost cold. 'Annie, that's a very serious allegation.'

Of course it's a serious allegation. It's the truth.

'I've got proof. I've read his diary . . .'

That's when I feel a heat rash cascading down my spine. The diary. You idiot, Annie! How could you let that slip? What if this gets back to the Sorrels?

'Annie?'

'They were bullying him.'

A moment's silence, then an admission that hits me like a battering ram:

'I know.'

'But a moment ago . . . '

'I know John was being bullied,' she says. 'Mrs Kruger was the first to spot it. She asked me to look into it. I was the one who referred it to Mr Storey.'

Everything I've been led to believe is suddenly called into question. Can it really be true? John didn't once mention a teacher being involved, though I suppose it makes sense. How else would Mr Storey get to know?

'You did?'

Mrs Linklater meets my wide-eyed stare. 'I'd suspected for a while. A few years' teaching and you get a nose for this sort of thing. John seemed very depressed so I challenged him about it. Getting him to open up was like cracking a safe.'

Somehow, that rings true. So many times I asked John about the teachers. So many times he dismissed my question. They didn't help. Nobody did. It was all about him: how he could take it, how he could survive.

'What happened?' I ask, suddenly confused.

'Mr Storey interviewed John. After that, he spoke to the four boys and their parents. They admitted to a bit of teasing . . .'

'Teasing!' I cry. 'It was a lot more than that.'

'You might be right, Annie, but John was hardly helpful. Maybe he was worried about recriminations.'

She hesitates, murmuring something about his broken tooth, then continues: 'I don't know what John was thinking, to be honest. He was never the most forthcoming boy at the best of times. He was uncooperative, quite sullen really. You would have thought we were taking the other boys' side, the way he gave us the cold shoulder. To be honest, John acted as if it was him against the world. All he was interested in was getting out of Mr Storey's office.'

'So nothing was done?'

'To the other boys, you mean?'

I nod.

'There wasn't that much we could do, Annie. John wouldn't come up with any serious allegations. Even with his mother present, he wouldn't open up.'

Why doesn't that surprise me? And what did you do, Mrs Linklater? Nothing, I bet, as usual.

'Mr Storey spoke to the other lads, of course,' Mrs Linklater resumes. 'He tried to warn them off. He also told the staff to keep an eye on John. He made a point of it in morning briefing. Oh, and Mrs Kruger barred the other boys from the library at lunchtime.' Her voice falters. 'In light of what happened, maybe we should have done more.'

For weeks I've been preparing myself for this moment. I imagined self-righteous anger. It doesn't come. Suddenly getting justice for John has become more complicated than I ever expected.

from John's diary
Monday, 28th April

Back in school.

Mocks, hiding in the library at lunchtime, the Gang of Four.

How depressing does that sound?

Today was a quiet day. Almost a happy day. I like that phrase. I stole it from the writer Alexander Solzhenitsyn. His *One Day in the Life of Ivan Denisovich* is my favourite book, one man's quiet struggle for survival. You should have seen the look on the faces of the Gang of Four when they caught me reading that one. I was in the LRC. It was just before Mr Storey had us all in his office and barred them from coming in the building at lunchtime.

'Well, if it isn't John Sorrow,' Fraser chuckled.

They've been calling me that since March. It's taken over from Joanne. That's about the extent of their wit.

'A day in the life of who?' said Okey, reading the title of my book.

It was as if the title of the book was meant as a calculated insult. I almost felt sorry for him. It can't be good, standing there with your lobotomy showing.

'Ivan Denisovich,' I replied, my voice flat and dull with resentment. 'It's Russian.'

'Why don't you read something English?' was Woodford's contribution, 'something normal?'

Normal, that's his favourite word. Strange how, in his world, it's normal to pinch and punch, name-call and bully, cover somebody's face with stolen make-up or strap a bra on them, but it's not normal to read a Russian novel. I hate him so much. I hate his hard, black little eyes. They remind me of mouse droppings. I hate his pinched features and his pointed nose. I hate his half-moustache. I hate his stupidity. Yes, and I hate his mocking laugh. That more than anything. Laughter should be the most beautiful thing in the world. It is with Annie. Woodford's laugh is different. It gets under your skin like a surgeon's scalpel, cutting and probing. It digs and slides and punctures. It's a weapon.

'What's normal?' I snapped, braver than usual. 'The *Sun*?'

That annoyed Woodford, especially when Okey snorted out a chuckle.

'Are you calling me thick?' Woodford said.

Seeing the look in his mouse-dropping eyes, my rare display of courage evaporated.

'No,' I said. 'Of course not.'

He looked around for Mrs Kruger. Satisfied she'd popped out for a moment, he snatched the book out of my hand.

'Hey,' I cried. 'Give it back!'

'Not till you eat your words, John Sorrow.'

That's when I understood.

Woodford nodded at Rice. Rice took the door. Okey and Fraser grabbed my arms. That's when Woodford did it. He started ripping pages out of the book and stuffing them into my mouth. I struggled and clamped my jaws shut. It didn't do any good. It just made them twist and pull at my face until they forced my mouth open. Then I was gagging, retching and choking on the crumpled paper being poked between my lips. I tried to fight my way free.

'Eat up, gay boy,' said Woodford.

I fought. At least, I did my best to fight. I managed to jab my elbow into Fraser's face but that didn't even slow them down. Soon I could feel my own saliva running down my chin. I knew it would be mixed with newsprint, grey saliva staining my shirt. I gargled out a cry: 'Get off me!'

All they did was shove more in and all the while they were laughing. Finally Rice hissed a warning. 'Here's Kruger.'

Then they were gone. Hearing Mrs Kruger's heels clicking in the corridor, I hurriedly spat the paper into the bin. When she came in I was wiping my face with a tissue.

'Are you OK, John?' she asked.

'Yes. Why?'

'You look a little peaky.'

Peaky? Peaky! Didn't she have any idea what they were doing to me? Couldn't she imagine the humiliation I'd just suffered? She shot a suspicious look down the corridor.

'It didn't have anything to do with those boys, did it?'

'Leave it, eh?' was all I could bring myself to say.

'John, if they're upsetting you, you've only got to say.'

Peaky, upsetting, where does she get this stuff from? We're not living in a costume drama. This is real life, ugly, mean, foul-mouthed. Plus there'll be more to come if I grass them up.

'Leave it,' I said. 'Please.'

'But John . . .'

'Oh, have it your own way!' I snapped, shoving back my chair and heading for the door.

She called after me, begging me not to go. I took no notice. What if I did complain? Did she really think it would make any difference? I did say something, of course, not long after that incident. The Gang of Four didn't stop. They just found a different way to get at me.

Today, though, there has been nothing. The only one I've bumped into was Rice. He hardly paid me any attention at all. To be honest, out of the four of them, he's the only one who seemed the slightest bit worried by Mr Storey's little talk. Rice has half a brain, which is half a brain more than any of the losers he hangs around with. He's even in top set for a couple of subjects. He's got something to lose.

Annie

We're going to see *Macbeth* this Friday. It's on at the Playhouse. Normally, I'd be looking forward to it but it reminds me that we're carrying on with our own version in Drama and that means having to partner Matthew again. Mrs Linklater (there, got it right first time) has just spoken to me again. I told her what the Gang of Four had been doing to John. I could tell by the look on her face she didn't know the half of it.

'Why didn't John say something? Mr Storey gave him four or five opportunities to speak.'

'Maybe he thought it would just make things worse,' I suggested.

'But we made it clear we would act on any new incidents.'

'When it'd been going on that long, I don't think he trusted anybody. Besides ... '

'What?'

I wondered how to put it. 'John was like that, moody. I think he'd resigned himself to the bullying. He took it as some kind of test, a rite of passage. He was just going to put up with it until he could get away to university.'

'But that's terrible,' said Mrs Linklater. 'How can you write off two years of your life?'

I thought of John and that family of his. Maybe it was more than two years he was writing off.

'John lived inside his imagination,' I said, though my explanation begged more questions than it answered. 'He called it his citadel. As long as he could do that, he was safe.'

'So what happened?' Mrs Linklater asked. 'If he had put up with it all this time, what broke him? What was the final straw?'

98

All I could do was stare back at her. She was right. There had to be a trigger. But what? I didn't know. I've been asking myself the same question since America. What brought down the citadel walls? I got up to go but Mrs Linklater wasn't finished.

'Just one more thing, Annie,' she said. 'What about you and Matthew?'

'What about us?'

'I was going to put on a production of our version of *Macbeth*. Mr Storey's sold on it.'

'And you want me to play Lady Macbeth to Matthew's Macbeth?'

'That's about the size of it. What do you think?'

'I think,' I said slowly, 'that you're expecting too much.'

I could hardly believe what I was saying. A year ago I'd have been all: *yes, Miss, no, Miss*. I'm turning into a real tough cookie. She sighed.

'So that's a no?'

I rolled my eyes. 'Of course it's a no. It would mean betraying John's memory.'

'Matthew isn't a bad lad,' Mrs Linklater said. 'Just a bit weak, that's all, easily led. I know for a fact he made an effort to steer clear of John after the interview with Mr Storey.'

I nodded. That was in John's diary. It was something, I suppose, but nowhere near enough.

'But it doesn't make any difference?'

I shook my head fiercely. 'How could it? All that time he went along with the bullying. I can't just forget all about it, can I?'

Mrs Linklater gave the slightest of nods. Leaving her to her marking, I go in search of Bryony. I find her in the canteen with Joanne, Shobna and Kelly. I hear their laughter and immediately feel out on a limb. The way Bryony looks up I know she's going to ask what Mrs Linklater wanted. I warn her off with my eyes and she takes the hint.

'Anything you'd like to tell us about you and Matthew?' Shobna asks.

'I beg your pardon?'

'You and Matthew. All that stuff at the Mega-Bowl and now

you're paired up together in Drama.'

I glare at Bryony and she drops her eyes. 'It was a one-off,' I say. 'I couldn't get out of it.'

Joanne giggles. 'Are you sure you really tried?'

'Oh, stop it,' I snap. 'I wouldn't have anything to do with Matthew Rice if he was the last boy on earth.'

'Annie,' Joanne says, 'don't you think you might be protesting a bit too much?'

'You don't get it, do you?' I say. 'Matthew made John's life a misery.'

'So you keep saying,' Kelly says in that bored-sounding way of hers. What she means by those four little words is: *do stop going on*. Well, Kelly, I don't intend to stop. What I actually say is:

'There's nothing between Matthew and me. Do you want me to spell it out for you? I can't stand him.'

Luckily it's the reading group in ten minutes and I have an excuse to get away from Joanne, Kelly and Shobna. I set off in the direction of the library with Bryony.

'Why did you have to tell them what happened in Drama?' I say. 'You know what they're like.'

'Sorry.' Bryony actually looks sorry.

'OK, let's forget it.'

'So what did Mrs Linklater want?'

'Guess.'

'I assume it was about Matthew,' Bryony says. 'What him and the others did to John.'

'Got it in one.'

'So?'

'So nothing. I told her what they'd done. She was shocked but she gave me the impression there's nothing further that can be done.'

Bryony plucks a wisp of hair from the corner of her mouth. 'That's true, isn't it?'

'As far as the school's concerned, it is.'

'But not for you?' says Bryony.

'No,' I answer. 'Not for me.'

We turn the corner. The LRC is in front of us.

'There was one more thing.'

'What's that?'

'She's doing a performance of that new version of *Macbeth*. She wanted me and Matthew in the lead roles.'

'So what did you say?'

I stop and stare at her. 'What do you think I said? I refused.'

Bryony's eyes light up. 'So there's an opening for somebody else?'

Then I understand. 'Bryony, promise me you won't take the part if you're asked. Promise,' I insist. 'If we're to be friends, you have to do this for me.'

Eventually Bryony nods her agreement. 'I promise.'

I enjoy the reading club. It's a welcome escape from the Gang of Four and the talk about Matthew and me. We're reading *To Kill a Mockingbird*. Bryony draws our attention to the chapter where the kids start finding objects in a knot hole, left by the mysterious Boo Radley. John talked about it while we were in Florida. He liked that kind of stuff: secrets, codes, hidden messages. My attention slips away from the discussion. It's just the kind of thing John would do, leave stuff in a knot hole to be found. That thing he said about his window seat, how he would leave messages in it, that was just like Boo Radley.

'So what do you think, Annie?' somebody asks. 'About Boo Radley.'

'Oh, well he's the mockingbird, isn't he, at least one of them?'

That sets off another discussion. I don't join in. I'm too busy thinking about John. Why didn't you leave me a message? Why didn't you tell me what pushed you over the edge?

from John's diary
Friday, 2nd May

All good things have to come to an end. By good things, I mean four days that were virtually torment-free – almost happy, if you like. Mum had even noticed the change in me.

'That holiday's done us all the power of good,' she said last night.

The power of good. What a wonderful world it would be if those words really meant anything, if there were some power of good which would descend from on high and smite down the wrongdoer. But this is reality. I've stopped believing in the power of good. I believe in the power of endurance.

Lowering her voice, Mum added: 'Those boys, they have been leaving you alone, haven't they?'

I told her, yes, those boys were leaving me alone. It was true, for the last few days. But today it all kicked off again. The truce was over. I should have told Mum. But how could I? She was so desperate to believe things were getting better, I didn't have the heart to tell her the truth. I was so glad to see her smiling, to have my mum back, that I allowed myself this little white lie.

I knew they would find a new way to get back at me and they have. It came in the form of a text message. Hardly original: I've seen it on the TV news, virtual bullying they called it. Old hat, but it did the job. They cornered Peter the other day in the yard and got the number from him. He's scared stiff of the Gang of Four. He keeps apologising for handing over my number, but I tell him to forget it. I don't want to fall out with him over it. After all, he's about the only friend I've got at Grovemount. This is what the text said:

Don't get too comfortable, you little bitch.
You can run but you can't hide.

I stood by the bus stop, staring at it as if there would be more. Bitch, that's what they called me. Ever since they started calling me gay, they've come up with a whole glossary. I felt a lump of nausea rising in my throat. If they could talk like this to me, how would they treat somebody who really was gay? My four days of peace made the renewal of hostilities an even more bitter pill to swallow. I found myself looking around. Were they watching me, gauging the message's effect? I didn't see them but that didn't mean they weren't around. I was about to put the mobile away when I got another text. Just one word:

Queer.

I was still staring at it when I heard footsteps. It was Matthew Rice. He was on his own. For a second I met his gaze. It was just a second. I've learned not to provoke the Gang of Four by eye contact. You'd have sworn he knew nothing about the text. The bus was a long time coming. I could almost feel my flesh crawling, standing as I was just a few metres away from one of my main tormentors. Any minute the rest of the gang was bound to arrive. That's what all this was about, wasn't it? Rice was the one sent to check on my reaction, to have a good laugh at my expense. I found myself stealing a glance at him. Guess what, he was already staring in my direction.

'You've no need to be worried,' he said.

Just like that, I had no need to be worried! 'What?'

'I'm not going to pick on you any more.'

I still had the mobile in my hand. What was this, some sort of wind-up?

'Sure,' I answered. 'Like I'm going to believe you.'

'You should,' said Rice. 'It's the truth.'

Oh, you're good, I thought, sincerity dripping from every pore. Except I know what you're up to.

'My folks went mad at me after old man Storey dragged them

103

in,' he continued. 'My dad's a solicitor, for God's sake. Imagine how it would look for him, me suspended from school. They grounded me for a week.'

'What do you want from me?' I asked, still aware of the mobile in my hand. 'Sympathy?' Every word, every breath oozed contempt for him. I saw a little light die away in his eyes, the snuffing of a candle of hope.

'Of course not,' he said, sounding weary. 'I saw you looking at me, that's all. I just wanted to say, if anything else happens, it isn't down to me. I can't afford any more trouble.' He held out his hand. No, I'm not kidding, Matthew Rice actually wanted to shake hands. Some of the other kids were staring at us. 'No hard feelings,' he said. 'Truce.'

Me, I stared at the hand. I know this scene, I thought. I take his hand and Woodford, Fraser and Okey jump out from somewhere, laughing themselves sick.

Well, this is one fall guy who isn't about to go along with the joke. 'You must think I was born yesterday,' I said. Same sourness in my voice. Same contempt.

That's when the bus came. Without another word to Rice, I climbed on board.

Hands

Hands of friendship,
helping hands,
hands
to lend,
hands up,
hands off,
hands that are shaken
or,
just by themselves
shake with fear.
Hands made of
four fingers,
a thumb
and a palm,
balled into a fist,
hands made
to do me harm.

Annie

Thursday, 18th September

Even when I'm supposed to be working, even in the middle of coursework, John is always there. I've been at the computer for an hour when something takes hold of me. Maybe it's a change in the lighting in the room. Maybe it's a snatch of a song on the radio. Whatever it is, something reminds me of John. I find myself thinking about him. It's almost as if I can feel his breath on my cheek, the way I did that day at the villa. He's so real, so . . . *here*, yet he's gone. Then I'm trawling through the e-mails, searching for something of him, trying to re-create him in my mind: his voice, his eyes, his warm, loving presence. Though I know most of the things he wrote by heart, I read every single one. When I think about the e-mails I exchanged with him I wonder if I could have done more. Did I say the right things? Could I have been more persuasive? It's not that I feel guilty, no that's not it. Not really. It's worse than that. I feel . . . helpless. I found this one in the deleted items:

> From: john450@yellowbrickroad.co.uk
> To: anniec@maplenet.ca
> Date: May 2nd 18:34
>
> Annie,
> I miss you like crazy.
> You can't imagine what it's like to be back.
> Nothing's changed. They were all waiting for
> me, lined up like crows on a fence. Do you
> know the Prometheus story? The gods send a
> bird to feed on his living flesh. That's the

way I feel. They've taken to calling me John
Sorrow. Heard about the shortest book in the
world? It's called: 'The wit and wisdom of
the Gang of Four'. Oh, they came up with a
new trick today but I wasn't falling for it.
Rice was the one who tried to con me. Do you
know what he did? He tried to get me to shake
hands. Can you imagine it? I told him where
to get off.
All the way home on the bus the sun was in my
face, flashing through the treetops at the
side of the road. I closed my eyes and felt
the warmth on my skin. I tried to imagine
myself back in Florida, close to you.
It's all such a long way from here.
Love,
John

I'd replied straight away, begged him to tell the teachers. It
made me so angry, thinking of him being pursued by those . . .
animals. I couldn't stand the idea of him muddling through,
taking it. But what do most people do in life? They go through
the motions. They hang on in there, so they can raise their families, so they can get by. I watch them on my way to school: the
kids on the bus; the office workers in their traffic jams; mums
pushing their little ones in their buggies; pensioners queuing
outside the post office, waiting for it to open. It seems to be
what makes the world go round, the ability to hold on.

Everywhere you look there are thousands of people making
do, getting by. Then, every once in a while, there is somebody
like John, somebody who can't do it any longer. You hear them
break, like a precious vase dropped during an auction. People
look away, embarrassed.

When I came back from Canada I swore I would be the one
who didn't look away. I made a promise to John's memory. I
haven't got justice, though. Sure, Matthew has made some kind
of apology, or at least he has said he wasn't the main one doing

it. As for the others, especially Luke, they haven't said a word. Nothing that I have said or done has so much as made them flinch. Meanwhile, everything goes on as normal. We go to school, we do homework, we go on trips . . .

Trips. That's it. Tomorrow we go to the theatre. Macbeth will cower before the ghost of Banquo. Lady Macbeth will try to scrub the stain of blood from her hands. That's it. I know how to get justice for John.

from John's diary
Monday, 5th May

Bank holiday Monday.

I've left my mobile off. Why let them spoil today? I don't have to go to school. I don't have to see them. I don't have to hide from them. So why leave my phone on so they can get to me that way?

Stress Hound came out with a corker today.

'When you're young, you think you're invincible.'

Really? Well, I'm young and I feel utterly vincible – is that a word? If you can be invincible, why can't you be vincible? Anyway, I've never felt fireproof or impregnable once in my whole life. What makes some people thick-skinned and impervious to pain while others are sensitive to every hurtful word, wounded by every hostile stare? Why are some people paper and others scissors? Could be it's in the genes. Genetically, I'm a victim.

This afternoon I found myself watching Katie playing. All her life, she's been a happy, well-balanced child. I've always had a love–hate relationship with her. That's nothing unusual, I suppose. It's the way it's supposed to be between brothers and sisters, isn't it, the old sibling rivalry? But how come, even on her worst days when she was little more than a palette of dirt, snot and tears, she always came up smiling, until now she's the golden child, all sunny dis-position and sparkling eyes? I just don't get it. Why is she happy and I'm not? She caught me looking at her.

'What are you staring at?'

'Nothing.'

'Well stop it. You're freaking me out.'

I let her be. A few minutes later Stress Hound joined her in the garden. It wasn't long before he was throwing her up in the air and she was giggling fit to burst. Funny thing, I don't remember him ever doing that with me. Katie's the apple of his eye. He's the same with Jessica. His love for them just comes bubbling out of him. Is it because I'm a boy? Is that it? I don't see it somehow. You see other dads with their sons, having fun. For some reason he's never felt the same about me. I caught him on holiday, the time he saw me shaking my booty (doesn't that sound ridiculous now?). He only mouthed it, but I read his lips.

'Freak of nature.'

What kind of man calls his son a freak of nature? What kind of dad is that?

Annie

Friday, 19th September

'Oh Annie, I'm so pleased!'

I've just told Mrs Linklater that I'll play the female lead in her play after all. That's her reaction. Bryony is walking alongside us from the coach to the school's main entrance. It's hard to read her expression. Shock, suspicion, maybe even a touch of horror, they're all there. One thing's for certain, she knows I'm up to something.

'So what made you change your mind?' Mrs Linklater asks.

She'd like to think it was her. Teachers like Mrs Linklater have this missionary thing. They're out to save souls. Don't flatter yourself, Mrs L. Much as I've always liked and admired you, you don't have the words to make me change my mind over this. By way of reply, I shrug my shoulders.

'Anyway,' Mrs Linklater says. 'So long as we can get on with our production. You really are the best person for the part.'

She notices Bryony. 'If that's all right with you, Bryony.'

'Sure, I don't mind.' Bryony's eyes are still fixed on me. I know that, the moment I'm finished with Mrs Linklater, I'm in for an interrogation. I put it off for as long as possible. Eventually however, it's time to face the music.

'OK, Annie,' Bryony says, following me out of the school gates. 'What's the game?'

I shift my gaze to a point on the horizon. 'I don't know what you mean.'

'Yes you do. Yesterday you were making me promise I wouldn't take the part. Now you've got it for yourself. What are you up to?'

'Bryony, you're paranoid.'

'Am I? So why don't you give me a straight answer?'

We're at the bus stop. I stand, still half-turned away from her, looking up the road. I don't reply.

'This is all about John, isn't it?'

'What if it is?'

There's desperation in Bryony's voice. 'Annie, think about this, will you? If you make a scene . . .'

'Bryony,' I say. 'It's a play. I'm supposed to make a scene.' Flippant, or what?

'Oh, don't play games,' she says, grimacing with disappointment at my words. 'You know exactly what I'm saying.'

We're interrupted by Matthew's arrival. He looks flushed and excited.

'Annie,' he says. 'Does this mean we're OK?' He doesn't say *forgiven*.

'Yes,' I answer. 'We're OK.'

The bus is pulling up.

'Do you mind if I sit with you?' he says. He glances at Bryony. 'If that's all right with you, Bryony.'

Bryony makes a noise, somewhere between a sigh and a snort. Everybody's asking her that today. She notices Kelly and Shobna jogging towards us.

'Yes, that's fine. My friends are here.' Fixing me with a last, glacial stare, she pushes ahead of us onto the bus, leaving me to slide in next to Matthew halfway down. His forearm brushes mine. In spite of myself I feel a shudder of excitement. He makes my skin tingle. I want to run and scrub away the sensation. What's wrong with me? Why do I betray John every time Matthew so much as comes near me?

'I'm glad it's all over,' he says, 'you know, that stuff with John.' He turns to look at me. I look straight ahead, fighting with my thoughts.

'I know Luke went a bit too far sometimes,' he says. 'But there has to be more to it than a bit of teasing. John was always a bit of an oddball, wasn't he?'

He senses me stiffen.

'Sorry, I didn't mean oddball,' he says. 'No, what I mean is, he was a loner. He was always a bit on the depressive side.'

I can't keep quiet any longer. 'So you had to push him to the brink?'

'Annie, that isn't what happened. You should have seen him. He didn't just lie down and . . . ' He winces at the thought of what he was about to say. 'He didn't give in. He stuck up for himself. I even thought he was getting a bit cocky, telling us he was fireproof, we couldn't touch him.'

'He said that?'

Matthew nods. 'Yes, word for word.'

I feel his touch on the back of my hand. An electric charge is flowing down my arm, pulsating through every nerve. No, not this. I don't need this complication.

'Annie,' Matthew says, his voice dropping to a hush, 'you must know I like you.'

I snatch my hand away. 'Yes, and you've got to know it's never going to happen.'

Matthew looks confused. Isn't that just typical of his arrogance? He still thinks he's God's gift to the female sex. He really does believe, no matter what's happened, I'm going to be flattered by his intentions. What am I supposed to do, swoon at his feet?

'I thought we were OK,' he says.

'OK doesn't mean I want to go out with you.'

He tries to meet my gaze. 'Because of John?'

'Of course because of John,' I snap. 'What do you think? You give me the cow eyes and say a few weasel words and I'll forget all about him?'

'Annie,' Matthew says, 'I'm finding it hard to get my head round all this.'

I glimpse Bryony and the others watching me. It makes me even angrier with Matthew.

'Then stop trying,' I retort. 'Accept it for what it is. We're doing a play together and that's all there is to it.'

'And that's all there will ever be?'

I start to get up. 'This is my stop,' I tell him.

'Annie, is that all there will ever be?'

I pull away, forcing myself not to look at him. 'Yes, Matthew, that's all there will ever be.'

from John's diary
Tuesday, 6th May

Today they cornered me round the back of the school, where they store the big, steel wheelie bins. I virtually ran out of class, trying to reach the back door to the LRC, but they were too quick for me.

'Look,' I said, 'I don't want any trouble.'

'Then,' Woodford said, his usual sneer ruffling that ridiculous bum-fluff moustache, 'you shouldn't go round grassing people up to Storey.'

'Leave me alone,' I said. 'I won't go to him again. I promise. Anything, don't hurt me.'

'Bit late now, isn't it?' says Okey.

Fraser was a few metres away, acting as a look-out. Strangely, Rice was missing. What gives?

'What are you going to do?' I asked, unable to keep the shake out of my voice.

It was Woodford who answered. 'Wouldn't you like to know, gay boy?'

He took a step forward and I flinched. I couldn't stop myself raising my right leg in a feeble attempt at self defence.

'Look at the little bitch,' he laughed, doing the limp-wristed bit. 'Ooh, don't hit me, you bad boy.'

That's when I snapped. 'Stop calling me that!' I yelled.

Woodford grabbed my jaw and squeezed, forcing my mouth open. 'Don't you dare raise your voice to me, gay boy.'

I was still struggling.

'Do you want us to make you eat your words again?' he asked.

I managed a last gesture of defiance. 'Drop dead.'

Luke tightened his grip, making me cry out in pain.

'Let me go!'

'Hear that, boys? The gay boy wants us to let him go.'

'Look,' I said, fighting to steady the quiver in my voice. 'Why do you keep calling me that? You're being stupid. I'm not gay.' Then I blurted it out, probably the most stupid thing I've ever said in my whole life. 'I haven't got a gay bone in my body.'

Well, they loved that.

'Gay bones!' Woodford roared. 'Oh, that's good that is. That explains it, doesn't it, the little bitch has got gay bones.'

So Okey joined in. 'Yes, I bet they even show up pink on the X-ray.'

Then Okey and Fraser started singing their stupid little ditty: 'Dem bones, dem bones, dem pink bones . . . '

Woodford still had hold of me. I managed to prise his hand away from my face and squirmed free.

'Get away from me!' I cried. It was almost a scream. They didn't stop, of course. They just set up this chorus:

'Ooh, get away, get away.'

I tried to get past but they kept blocking my escape. That's when one of the lunch-time supervisors saw us.

'Hey!' she called. 'You're not supposed to be round there. Get back in the yard.'

'Catch you later, John Sorrow,' said Woodford. 'Oh yes, and keep your mobile switched on.'

I watched them go, then walked past the supervisor, head down.

'Are you all right, son?' she asked.

'Sure,' I replied. 'Why wouldn't I be?'

With that, I opened the door to the LRC. Mrs Kruger asked me if there was something wrong. I didn't answer.

Annie

Saturday, 20th September

I'm babysitting again. It's getting to be a bit of a routine, and not one I enjoy. But for John's diary, I wouldn't set foot in this house again. There's a deep coldness built into the bricks of the place. I don't feel comfortable. I don't understand the Sorrels' social whirl either. For starters, I'm not sure Mrs Sorrel's that keen on going out at all. She certainly doesn't look happy. It's Mr Sorrel. He's the one. He seems determined to help her to get over John's death. It's as if he thinks he's got to keep her occupied. What is it people always say? She's got to take her mind off it. I don't know, there are times I think he wants her to forget John altogether. No, that's a terrible thing to say. He could be hard on John, but he was still his father.

Lauren's staying over again. That's another routine. They're driving me mad tonight. They're both as high as kites. It's going to be really late before I can go back to John's diary. I've read it very nearly to the end, but still there's something I don't understand. There's something missing: a reason. To kill yourself, surely there's got to be a turning point, something that takes you over the top. That's what I can't square to myself at all. He didn't even leave a note. Isn't there always meant to be a note? I've looked for something in his diary, something around the time he did it. He took the pills on May 11th but there's no entry for that date. How come? Why this sudden act? Even when John was telling me about the bullying, I always got the feeling he could cope. Deep inside, he knew they weren't worth the dirt on his shoes. There's more to it. I know there is.

'Annie,' Lauren shouts. 'We're going round next door to play with Rebecca.'

My heart skips a beat. This is my chance. But what would the Sorrels think? Should I let them go?

'I don't know,' I say.

'Oh, go on, Annie. We've got our mobiles. And we're going to be indoors the whole time. Rebecca's got this really great DVD we want to watch.'

'How long is it?' I ask.

'Don't know. We'll still be back before nine o'clock.'

'Isn't it going to be dark by then?' I say.

'Not very,' says Katie hopefully.

That's when the idea comes to me, the way I can keep them out of my hair while I read the diary.

'I can't let you come home in the dark,' I say. 'Not even from next door. Tell you what, I'll come and get you at nine.'

'So we can go?' says Lauren.

'Yes, you can go.'

'Thanks,' says Lauren. 'You're the best.'

They're at the door when Katie stops. 'Oh, I forgot to tell you,' she says. 'Jessica phoned for Mum.'

'Jessica?'

'My big sister.'

That's right. John mentioned her. Jessica. She's a student somewhere. Katie says something else, something I don't quite catch.

'If she calls again,' I call after her, 'I'll take a message.'

But she's already gone. I walk to the front window and watch them all the way to the neighbours' front door where they are met by a chubby, dark-haired girl. She must be Rebecca. Satisfied that they are not coming back, I jog upstairs to John's room. Darting a glance at Kurt Cobain, I take out John's diary. Quickly, I read to the end, the entries he wrote just a few days before his death. There's still the same nagging feeling. Something's missing. I find myself re-reading each entry. That's when I notice something. The diary doesn't feel right. I squeeze it. I turn it over and look at the binding. Sure enough, several pages have been removed. Not individual pages either. The book is bound in fifteen or twenty sections. A few pages have been eased out, so carefully I hadn't noticed until now, but there is definitely a gap in the binding.

'Could that be the May entries,' I wonder out loud, 'the missing ones? But why remove them, and where are they now?'

It doesn't make sense. He was so fussy about his things, especially books. He winced when he saw people bending books back. He said it broke the spines. So why would he do this to his precious diary? But the book refuses to offer up its secrets. I'm sitting cross-legged on the floor, staring at the pages and puzzling over the missing pages, when the phone rings. I race downstairs.

'Yes?'

'Annie? You sound out of breath.' It's Mrs Sorrel.

'I was playing music. I must have had it on a bit loud.'

'Not too loud, I hope.'

'Oh no, don't worry about that, Mrs Sorrel. I'm not going to annoy the neighbours or anything.'

'I'm sure you aren't,' she says. 'You're such a sensible girl. Are the girls all right?'

'Yes, fine. I hope you don't mind. I let them go next door until nine o'clock. They're watching a film with Rebecca. They've got their mobiles and I'm going round for them at nine. I won't let them stay too long.' I realise I'm trying way too hard to sound responsible.

'No problem at all, Annie,' Mrs Sorrel says. 'I was only phoning to tell you our older daughter Jessica might be calling.'

'Yes, Katie told me.'

'Oh, I didn't think she'd remember.'

'Do you want me to give her a message?' I ask.

'No need,' Mrs Sorrel says. She says a couple of other things but I'm hardly listening. I just want to get her off the phone.

'Right,' she says finally, 'that's all I was phoning for. See you later.'

'Yes, see you.'

I put down the phone and go back to John's room. For half an hour I just flick back and forth through the diary. There's got to be something in those pages, something from the days leading up to May 11th, but where are they?

'Oh John, why did you have to be like this?' I say. 'Why did you have to hide everything?'

It was the way he didn't tell the teachers about the bullying, the way he kept quiet to his parents. If only he'd shared what was happening to him, then maybe the citadel wouldn't have crumbled.

'Is there more?' I murmur. 'What did you write in the pages you removed?'

Defeated, I get up off the floor. I find myself staring at the computer screen.

I check the time. It's half past eight. I've got time to look at his files before I have to go for the girls. I sit drumming my fingers on the computer table.

'Oh, come on.' Then the desktop appears. I browse through My Documents. Nothing. So I click on Internet Explorer. 'Come on.' Finally, I'm scrolling through the sent items. There it is:

```
From: john450@yellowbrickroad.co.uk
To:   anniec@maplenet.ca
Date: May 6th 20.05

Annie,
They won't stop. They just won't stop. I
promised to hold on but I just don't know how
any more. The citadel walls are cracking and
the attack has come from within. Nobody
cares. Only you. Annie, my lovely Annie,
you're the only one who cares. You're the
only one who will know how to find out what's
happened to me.
Love always,
John
```

'I will know,' I say, my voice echoing strangely in the empty room. 'You said I will know. I didn't get that the first time I read it.'

I sit staring at the screen. 'I still don't understand.'

What did he mean? How will I ever find out? I stare at the

diary with its torn out pages. I stare at the computer screen. It's ten to nine. I'll have to go for the girls soon. I hear John's voice running through my mind, as clear as if he were sitting here next to me. I hear him talking about his hopes and dreams. I rerun all those conversations we had.

'Oh John,' I murmur. 'Why couldn't you hold on?'

And at long last I hear what he's saying. 'I would be like one of those romantic heroes hiding his diaries and letters in the window seat.'

A chill runs through me. Those missing pages, they'll tell me why he killed himself, they've got to. That's where I will find his innermost thoughts, the ones he couldn't put even in these pages, the ones he was hiding from the prying eyes of his mother when she was cleaning his room. He said *the* window seat. Not *a* window seat but *the* window seat, as if it really existed. When we were in Florida he always made out he had a hiding place, somewhere he could put things he didn't want his parents, especially his dad, to read. That's where the missing pages are going to be. But there is no window seat, nothing even remotely like one. The only window in John's bedroom is a small, double-glazed one. There's no seat, not even the space for a seat.

'I don't understand,' I groan out loud.

'I don't understand either,' a voice says behind me. 'I don't understand what you're doing in my brother's room.'

I spin round. There, in the doorway, a woman is watching me. She's in her early twenties. She's holding a cardboard box. I stare at her. I recognise the family features.

'You must be Jessica,' I say.

Now I understand. I thought Katie and Mrs Sorrel meant she was going to phone. No, they said she was going to *call*. Why didn't I listen properly?

'Well,' Jessica says. 'I'm waiting. What are you doing in John's room?'

'I didn't mean any harm,' I say. 'I just wanted to look round. I wanted to know why he did it. Jessica, I was his friend. I wanted to understand.'

I notice the clock on the wall. Even now, at this moment of

crisis, I can't forget my duties. 'Can I tell you everything in a moment?' I say. 'I've got to get the girls.'

'Where are they?' Jessica demands. She sounds cold, impatient.

I explain the girls' whereabouts.

'I'll get them,' Jessica says sharply. 'You're going to shut down the PC and put everything back the way it was, *exactly* the way it was. Do you understand?'

I nod miserably. 'I understand.'

from John's diary
Wednesday, 7th May

Why me?

Am I doing something wrong? I don't go looking for trouble. I don't ask for it. All I want is a bit of peace. All day long I try to be invisible. Every time I see the wolf pack I lower my eyes. It makes no difference. Still they come after me. Today I sat out in the garden for hours, just staring ahead. I couldn't read. I couldn't even think. That's what they do to me. They invade every part of my mind, burn their way into every atom of my being. I try to shut them out but still they penetrate my every waking moment. Even when they're not around I'm wondering when they'll appear next, or when they'll text me. Thanks to technology they can even do long-distance bullying. There's no hiding place.

Two more years after this one, that's what I keep telling myself, 24 months, 104 weeks. But two more years of *this*. It seems so little when you say it out loud. Two years to endure, less if they leave school after GCSEs, and there's every chance of that. That should be a comfort. But the way I feel right now I can't last another day. They're scaring me. Fear has become a rat eating through my heart, consuming everything else.

It's an odd thing. It begins in the morning. As soon as I wake up I'm aware of them. They're out there. I start wondering what they have in store for me. I imagine all the things they could do. The journey to school is the same. Even when they are out of sight, I can't get them out of my mind. I picture their faces in the dappled sunlight. Then, once I get to school, they don't have to do anything to scare me. Knowing that they could walk round any corner is enough. I never feel safe. And I'm so alone. I don't feel I can tell Mum. Dad will only talk her out of doing anything. I can hear him telling her it's no big deal, something lads go through. Peter's no use either. He's my friend out of school but, when we're there, he doesn't dare come near me. There's nobody I can turn to, nobody I can trust. I can never relax. I just want it to stop. I just want it to be over. There is a way, of course. There is always a way.

Annie

Sunday, 21st September

It feels as if the questioning is going to go on forever.

'Annie,' Mum says, 'whatever were you thinking of?'

'I told you,' I answer, silently willing her to let me be. 'I wanted to know why he did it.'

Mum is sitting next to me on my bed. Last night, face drawn and pale with disappointment, she sent me straight to my room. This is the first time we've spoken since then.

'You shouldn't have gone in his room like that. I mean, you read his diary. Annie, you betrayed their trust.'

I lower my eyes. 'I know.'

Last night was awful. Mrs Sorrel drove me home in silence. Her lips were pinched invisible. Lauren had her sleep-over cancelled, too. She sat in the back twisting the hem of her skirt. She was really upset. She kept staring at me, wondering what I had done and why she was being punished. Why wasn't I more careful? When they told me Jessica was going to call, I should have listened, taken time to understand. I was so eager to get my hands on the diary. Jessica was home for the weekend. She stays at her boyfriend's house when she's back. He still lives here. Just my luck. Now I'll never set foot in the Sorrel house again.

'Look,' Mum continues. 'I know you're upset about what happened to John but you've got to let it go.'

I want to argue back but it will only make things worse. 'I know.'

'When Mrs Sorrel brought you home, I didn't know what to say.'

I nod.

'It's so out of character, Annie. You've always been so sensible, so responsible. You've never given us a bit of trouble until this.'

Yes, that's me, everybody's good girl. But I don't want to be sensible, or responsible. I want to be at peace. I want to know why John did it, why, when he'd put up with it for so long. I want justice.

'It's been driving me mad,' I say. 'Not knowing why he did it.'

Mum sits down next to me and slips an arm round my shoulder. 'You know why, Annie. He was being bullied.'

'There's more to it,' I say.

Mum stiffens. She doesn't like the way this is going. 'Meaning?'

'I don't know, but something else was preying on his mind.'

Mum takes a deep breath. 'Maybe there was. Who knows what went on in that young man's mind? When I think back to Florida, maybe he was already suffering from depression. Denise struck me the same way. It could run in the family, couldn't it?'

'All the same,' I say, 'that isn't all it was . . .'

Mum interrupts me. She does it gently but she leaves me in no doubt that she wants me to drop it. 'The point is, Annie, we can't change what's happened. I know how you feel about John but you really do have to let it go.'

'I wasn't just being nosy, Mum,' I say. 'You must believe me. I wanted to understand, that's all. He was my friend.'

'That's right. He was your friend. *Was*. Life goes on, Annie. This might sound brutal but it's the living we have to care for now. Please listen to me, Annie. I know you're hurting but you've got to get through this.'

'I know,' I say, struggling to hold back my tears. 'I didn't want any of this to happen.' Before you know it I'm sobbing helplessly.

'I understand,' Mum says, giving me a hug and handing me a tissue. 'You're trying to be loyal.' She squeezes my shoulders. 'Even so, this can't go on. You see that, don't you?'

I've just about got the tears under control. I nod my agreement.

'I want to hear you say it, Annie.'

'I'm going to move on.'

'OK. Now dry your eyes.' She smiles. 'It's going to be all right, you know. Come on, let's go downstairs.'

'Mum, how do things stand with the Sorrels?'

She sighs. 'Pretty frosty. Anyway, let's try to put it behind us.'

End of conversation. We go downstairs. Dad looks disappointed. Lauren too. We eat in silence. At least, they eat. All I do is shove some Corn Flakes round the bowl with my spoon. When he's finished, Dad gets up. He's busy trying to make it up to Lauren.

'Do you want to go for a drive, Lauren?'

'Where?'

'I thought we could have a wander over the sand dunes, just you and me.'

'OK,' says Lauren. She follows him out of the room without so much as glancing at me.

'Looks like I'm still in the doghouse,' I say.

'It'll blow over,' Mum says.

If she knew what I was thinking she wouldn't let it go so easily. My promises are worthless. Even after all this, I can't give up. I've one more thing to do.

127

from John's diary
Thursday, 8th May

I won't be afraid any more. I won't beg. I won't plead. I won't hurt.
I will be strong.

Strong

The way the stars are bright,
The way the face in the mirror is mine,
The way the world turns, always turns,
The way a baby cries,
As sure as all of these,
The way the reed bends in the wind,
The way flesh returns to earth,
I will be what I must be.
I will be strong.

Annie

Monday, 22nd September

Bryony clears her throat. I know what's coming.

'Don't do it, Annie,' she says, leaning forward. 'Please.'

We're in the school yard, sitting on one of the graffiti-carved benches on the far side, by the railings. I run my hand over the gouged surface and, for a moment, I wonder about John's window seat and where it could be, or indeed, if it exists at all. Traffic rumbles by.

'Do what?' I ask.

A snort of impatience follows. 'You're my best friend, Annie, but I'm getting really fed up. Ever since you came back from Canada you're not the same person.'

I face her down with a long, cold stare. I'm in no mood for emotional blackmail or sentimentality. It isn't Canada that made the difference, and she knows it. It's John and what those boys did to him. She gets up to go. Try as I might to ignore my feelings, I call her back. I have so little now. Everything seems to have fallen apart. That's John's legacy. He has remade me in his own image. It's almost as if I am apart from the world now. Sometimes I wonder why it has to be like this. Why me?

'Bryony,' I say. 'Don't go.'

'So we're going to talk?' she says. 'More importantly, are you going to listen?'

'I'll listen.'

She joins me again on the bench. Her voice shrinks to a whisper. 'I know you're going to say something at the performance,' she says.

I slip back into hostile mode. 'Then you know more than I do.'

Bryony shakes her head. 'I thought we were going to talk.'

I stare ahead. It gives me no pleasure to act this way but how can I make her understand?

'We are talking,' I say.

'You're wrong, Annie,' Bryony says. 'I'm talking. You, you're playing games.'

Matthew is crossing the yard a few metres away. For a moment he glances our way. The way he looks at me, I could almost believe he knows what we're talking about. Bryony makes one last attempt to get through to me. I know how stubborn I'm being. I can't help it.

'Annie,' Bryony says. 'I'm going to ask you one last time. Are you going to say something at the performance?'

'No.'

This time, when she stands up, Bryony is in no mood to return. Giving me a look of resignation, she walks towards Shobna. I see the pair of them look over their shoulders at me. Suddenly I feel very alone. I've been sitting watching the crisp packets swirling round the litter bins for long, weary moments when I hear a voice. It's Naomi.

'Look at the sad, little cow,' she sneers to Luke.

He laughs. That's when I snap. It's the combination of Naomi's so-superior, high-pitched voice and Luke's knowing look that does it. I swear at them. Immediately, Naomi's expression changes. Gone is the mocking superiority. Her eyes flash.

'Take that back!' she shrieks, for all the world as if she has never heard bad language before.

Even now, I could back off. So far Naomi is only playing at anger. It's a minor wind-up. She is still prepared to walk away. So what do I do? I make it worse by bad-mouthing her again. Suddenly the world explodes. I'm on the floor. Naomi's on top of me, her hands twisting through my hair. My scalp is on fire. I can even feel her spittle spraying onto my face as she screams her anger. Under a barrage of abuse, I'm thrashing my head to and fro, trying as best I can to avoid her spit, her foul words. I'm kicking, not at her, just kicking, trying to break free. One of my shoes has come off. I know how stupid I must look with my skirt

130

halfway up my thighs and Naomi sitting astride me, tearing at my face and hair. She is stronger than me. This isn't the first time she's been in a fight. I'm trembling, gulping for air. Naomi slams my head against the ground and I feel sick. Sicker still when some of the Neanderthals in Year Nine come running.

'Catfight!'

I sense the press of bodies around us. Pinned as I am to the yard, I'm aware of the crowd, the heat of it, the hunger to see somebody humiliated. It's mostly boys. There is pain in this moment, but worse, there is shame. It's me they're looking at, *me*. All I can hear is those stupid male voices, laughing, chanting:

'Catfight!'

I'm so hot. I want to run my nails all over my skin, scrape away my humiliation. This is crazy. I'm on the ground, being scratched and punched, and all I care about is this overwhelming, choking heat.

'Get off me!'

That's my voice. It sounds alien but it's mine all right. More scream than yell, it echoes inside my head. Louder. 'Get off me!'

Then, in the blink of an eye, I'm being hauled to my feet.

'Are you OK, Annie?'

I find it hard to focus. Part of my face is numb. There is a pricking sensation on my lip just below the nostril, probably a trickle of blood. I'm vaguely aware of somebody's arms around me, bearing me away from the crowd. Then one of the lunch-time supervisors is there, appearing suddenly, a freeze-frame image of concern.

'What happened?' she says.

I manage a reply. 'I fell.' Sure, like she's going to believe that!

'What on?' she says. 'A bed of nails?'

Honestly, humour at a time like this.

'Who did this to you?' she asks.

Then my rescuer is speaking. 'She'll be OK. I'll take care of her.'

'I'm putting in a report,' the supervisor says stubbornly. 'The Head of Year's got to know.'

'Sure, whatever. Now will you leave me alone so I can take care of her?'

131

Reluctantly, the supervisor drifts away still muttering about the Head of Year. We've gone a few steps when I finally look up.

'Matthew!' A gasp of disgust, then: 'Take your hands off me.' I shove my hands against his chest and lever myself away from him.

'I'm only trying to help,' he tells me. There's a wounded look in his blue eyes.

'But I don't want your help, Matthew,' I retort, my voice combining shame, anger and despair in equal measure. I turn to go but there's Naomi and, next to her, Luke.

'You're not going to get anywhere with her, you know,' Luke chuckles. 'She hates your guts.'

Matthew's answer is brief and angry. 'Get stuffed!'

'You're losing it, Matt,' says Luke. 'You used to be a good laugh. You know your problem? You've forgotten who your friends are.'

Bewildered, I watch their quarrel. Even Naomi seems shocked by the ferocity of the exchange.

'Luke,' Matthew says, 'you're scum, plain and simple. I can't imagine what made me hang around with you so long. A friend like you I don't need.'

For a moment I think they're going to come to blows too. Then the tension breaks and I become aware of Bryony and Shobna.

'You need to get cleaned up,' Bryony says. 'The bell goes in ten minutes.'

I meet Matthew's eyes for a moment then look away, back at Bryony. 'I thought you'd given up on me.'

'I'm tempted sometimes,' she says, 'but no, for better or for worse, we're friends.'

from John's diary
Friday, 9th May

I know what to do. At last I have a purpose, a game plan. I'm not going to be a victim any more. I'm not going to take their crap. Life will be beautiful. There are people who care. There are! They can't turn away this time, not after this.

Not after this.

The Last Time

This will be the last time
I take it.
Seconds tick by.
The world outside of me,
Outside of my thoughts,
No longer has meaning.
Time shudders to a halt,
Implodes on itself.
The dog that leaps for the stick
Hangs in freeze-frame.
A single drop of water
Hangs suspended below the tap.
A salty tear waits,
Halfway through cutting a stream.
Down a cold cheek.
This will be the last time I cry.
This will be the last time.

Annie

Tuesday, 30th September

It's over a week since my fight with Naomi. Mrs Linklater knows all about it, of course. She got the lunchtime supervisor's report. She questioned me next day, just after registration, but I didn't tell her anything. I don't know why, to be honest. There was a time when I would have liked nothing better than to share my thoughts with her, my favourite teacher, my warrior queen. Somehow, I don't feel the need to share. I don't want protecting.

In spite of everything, I'm not afraid of Naomi. I almost feel sorry for her. Luke isn't going to make her happy. She'd do anything for him but he looks at other girls. All the time. I've seen him. I've spotted him chatting up Okey's younger sister, Siobhan. He isn't even subtle about it! Naomi still says things to me, mostly to impress Luke, but I ignore them. So, if I'm not scared of Naomi, why didn't I say anything to Mrs Linklater? Maybe I'm getting more like John. No, it's simple, really. It just doesn't have anything to do with her. This is about me.

The dress rehearsal is this Friday afternoon. Our whole year is going to watch. That's when I'm going to do it, that's when I'm going to tell the world what they did. The public performance would have been better, but since when does a knuckle-dragging moron like Luke Woodford go to plays? Anyway, I'm going to say *exactly* what they did, every detail. Bryony knows. She keeps trying to dissuade me but I change the subject. I don't know why she still wants to be my friend. I can't be much fun. She's always there, though, true as steel. When this is all over I'll make things up to her.

Katie came to the house for tea on Sunday. Her mum dropped her off. I was on my way round to Bryony's when they arrived.

We bumped into each other at the front gate. It made me feel a bit uncomfortable. Funnily enough, Mrs Sorrel seemed more embarrassed than I was. She could hardly look me in the eye. I haven't been round to babysit, of course, not since Jessica caught me in John's room that night. I thought she'd still be angry with me but she wasn't. It was almost as if she were the one who'd been caught doing something wrong.

'A penny for them,' Bryony says. We're in the library. Mrs Kruger's reading club has just finished.

'I beg your pardon?'

'You were on another planet,' Bryony explains.

'Oh.'

'Were you thinking about anything special?' she asks.

'No, nothing much.'

'Not John then, or Matthew?'

I frown. 'What makes you ask that?'

'He's thinking about you, Matthew I mean. He never takes his eyes off you.'

With a sigh I say: 'I know. It's creepy.'

'Why's it creepy?'

'Bryony, don't act simple. Because of what happened to John, that's why. You can't have forgotten that Matthew's one of the ones who did it.'

Bryony shakes her head. 'Not any more, he isn't. He doesn't have anything to do with Luke and the others. Everybody's talking about it.'

'It doesn't change anything though, does it?' I say. 'He helped to push John over the edge.'

'Are you sure about that?' Bryony asks. 'Really, really sure?'

'Yes,' I say. 'I'm sure. I know what he did.'

'You're being too hard on him,' Bryony insists. 'What do you want from him, Annie? He's said sorry for joining in the teasing. He's broken friends with Luke and the others. He's on his own now. Good God, he did it for you. Why can't you forgive him?'

With a shake of the head, I get up to go. 'We've got French in five minutes. Are you coming?'

Bryony nods and follows me.

That night I lie on my bed, fingers laced behind my head, staring at the ceiling. I think about John, not in a warm or fuzzy way, but the way he was: quiet, caring, vulnerable. At the thought of that afternoon at the villa, my skin starts to burn. I can feel his touch. It might be months ago but I can still sense the dark, prickling slide of unease as he runs his fingers over my damp throat. Do you know, it wasn't that I didn't want him touching me. There was more to it than that. Already, I felt as if I were betraying him. That's right, in being repelled by his touch, I was joining all the other people who let him down. John so desperately wanted to be loved, but I couldn't do that for him. Even worse, I couldn't even be honest about my feelings. So I stood there, holding my breath, until Mum arrived and I could escape.

'What's wrong with me?' I say out loud.

There is bitterness in those words. There is a lot more to this than the memory of John on that April day in Florida. Every time I remember his touch, I find myself thinking about other fingers, other hands. When I realised who had guided me away from Naomi, I had to force myself to push Matthew away. That's the problem. That really is the heart of it. When he held me, my skin burned, not with shame, not with embarrassment. My flesh sang. I wanted him to hold me. I didn't want it to end. Not ever.

Annie

Friday, 3rd October

It's today.

Halfway through brushing my teeth, I stare at myself in the bathroom mirror. For a moment my breathing is shallow. I can't do this, I tell myself, I can't fight the whole world. But the moment of surrender passes. I know I'm going to go through with it. Soon it will all be over. John will have closure and I will have peace. Mum and Dad will be devastated, of course. After what happened at the Sorrels, they are desperate for me to put it all behind me. They half-think I have. But they don't dare believe that it's completely out of my system, which is sensible when you think about it. Then there's school. If things have been tense since I confronted Matthew at the Mega-Bowl, imagine what it's going to be like after I accuse the boys, not in the hubbub of the bowling alley, not in a one-to-one confrontation, but in front of the whole year. I have to do this. For John. For me.

Bryony calls for me at a quarter past eight and we go for the bus together. She started coming round for me after the fight with Naomi. She wants to protect me. I think she's feeling a bit guilty that it was Matthew, not her, that came to my rescue. She's in a talkative mood, talkative even for Bryony. She rattles on about clothes, sisters, last night's TV, some stud whose latest movie is on at the multiplex, Shobna's new mobile. It's so good to be normal, frivolous, carefree that I have to tell her how glad I am she's my friend.

'You're great, you know that?'

The smile slips. 'Oh, don't go all sloppy on me, Annie.'

'I'm not. It's the truth. You're a good friend. The best.'

Look at her. She's embarrassed. In fact, she's gone positively gloomy. You'd think I'd insulted her, not paid her a compliment. Naomi gets on at the next stop. For once, there is no Luke. Just for a moment she pauses on her way down the bus, peering down at me, a half-smile playing on her lips. Then, without a word, she carries on to the back seat and sits exchanging noisy banter with her mates.

'What a performance,' Bryony comments.

She's right. The loud laughter is for my benefit, telling me I'm a sad little minger and she's the bee's knees.

'Ignore her,' I say. 'She isn't worth the effort.'

I trace a line in the condensation on the window and think of John's fingers running over my throat, then Matthew's squeezing my shoulder. How did things get like this?

The stop after Naomi, Matthew gets on. He's on his own. He's broken friends with Luke, Anthony and Michael all right. The four of them used to go everywhere together. All the seats have gone so he stands up. He seems very alone. I almost feel sorry for him. Twice I catch him staring at me.

'You could at least say hello,' Bryony observes. 'You're in the play together, after all.'

'It doesn't mean we have to be friends,' I retort.

Bryony catches Matthew's eye and shakes her head. For a moment, it is as if they are exchanging some sort of secret communication.

By lunchtime I can barely breathe. The dress rehearsal is first session this afternoon. In my mind's eye, I am up on that stage, jabbing an accusing finger at the boys, making my big speech. I've lain awake thinking about it. Now I feel sick to the pit of my stomach. Sure, I feel bad about doing this to Mrs Linklater, worse about hurting Mum and Dad, but this is my last, best chance to get justice for John. Goodness knows, I've put it off often enough.

'I've got to get changed in a minute,' I tell Bryony.

Dress rehearsal is a bit of a misnomer really. All we're doing is changing out of our school uniforms and into casual clothes.

'You've got plenty of time,' Bryony says.

'I haven't, you know,' I tell her.

But Bryony is looking past me. 'You've got all afternoon,' she says. 'The rehearsal is cancelled.'

I give her an uncomprehending stare. She could be talking fluent Armenian.

'Don't be daft.'

She continues to stare past me so I turn to see what she's looking at. To my surprise, there are Mrs Linklater, Luke, Anthony and Michael walking across the yard. I stare questioningly at Bryony. There's a kick in my chest. 'What's going on?'

'You've got what you wanted.'

Another kick. Dawning realisation too. It doesn't stop me asking her to explain. 'What do you mean?'

'Don't get angry,' she says.

I'm too bewildered to be angry. 'Bryony, what have you done?'

'I went to Matthew.'

Now I'm angry. I feel the burning flush on the back of my neck. 'You did what!'

'Annie,' she says, 'I had to. You know what it would do to your mum and dad if you caused a scene. And do you have any idea what it would do to you?'

I watch the three boys follow Mrs Linklater into school.

'Matthew went to Mr Storey at morning break,' Bryony explains. 'He's told him what they did, the whole thing, the way they tormented John.'

'You mean, the lies they told the police?' I snort. 'A bit of harmless skitting?'

'No,' Bryony says. 'The truth. Everything. Stuff you don't even know.'

I find myself thinking she doesn't have a clue what I know. Then I'm blinking hard, trying to get a handle on this.

'Annie,' she says. 'I should have listened to you earlier. I had a long talk with Matthew. He told me what they did. It was horrible. The way they pushed him into the girls' changing rooms.'

'What?'

Bryony hesitates.'Didn't you know? They stripped him and

140

pushed him into the girls' changing rooms. Fortunately for John there was nobody in at the time, but they weren't to know that.'

I thought of John crucified with embarrassment over his body. I remembered all the Joanne stuff.

'And you got Matthew to go to Mr Storey?'

Bryony shakes her head. 'That was his choice. He had nothing to do with the changing room thing. They were bragging about it all over the school, that's how he knew. Matthew was never as bad as the others. He'd do anything for you, even this.'

I should feel relieved, even grateful, but I don't. I feel disappointed, angry. This was down to me, nobody else. 'You went to Matthew behind my back,' I murmur. It's a statement of fact, not a question.

'You're not going to kick off on me, are you?' Bryony asks.

I stare straight ahead, trying to imagine what is going to be said in Mr Storey's office.

'Annie?'

Finally, I meet her eyes. She looks anxious. 'No,' I say wearily. 'I don't blame you for what you did.'

'So what are you going to do now?'

'Do? There's nothing to do.'

'I thought you'd go mad.'

I find myself smiling. 'You know what, Bryony, I think I've been mad for weeks. I can't say I'm delirious about what you did, but at least it's over. The people who didn't understand, they'll know John was driven to it. Everybody will know the truth.'

And that's what it's all been about, isn't it?

The truth.

Annie

Saturday, 4th October

I feel happier than I have for weeks.

'Hang on, Annie,' Dad calls from behind. 'We're not all as young as you.'

I don't want to hang on. I want to drive on up the path, drown my thoughts with the drumming pulse in my head.

'Annie, slow down.'

I stop and look back. Lauren has nearly caught up with me. Mum and Dad are toiling behind.

'It gets your heart thumping, doesn't it?' Dad pants.

It is the four-and-a-half-mile route round Ingleton waterfalls. We drove up this morning. Nurse Mum decided we needed the exercise. She's banned the salt cellar from the dinner table too. First the new treadmill in the spare room, now this. Operation Get Fit is in full swing. Mum hasn't been the same since she went on that last training day.

'Terrific sight, isn't it?' Dad says, looking at the clear water swirling over brown rocks.

'Yes,' I tell him. 'I'm glad we came.'

'We needed it,' Dad says, his voice dropping a tone. 'As a family.'

What he means is, they're claiming me back, for the family. Lauren is a little distance from the rest of us. It's her way of reminding everyone she wanted Katie to come too.

'Wait till you see round the next bend,' Dad says.

'You've been here before then?'

He glances back at Mum. 'Yes, when we were courting.'

'Courting?' I say. 'Dad, that was old-fashioned when you were . . .'

'Stepping out?' Dad suggests mischievously.

'Courting,' I say in mock resignation.

His surprise is a dramatic view over the hills.

'There you go,' Dad says.

There is barely a road, a house, a power line, never mind a town. It's easy to imagine Grovemount is a figment of the imagination. But I know better. There's been no news of Matthew and the rest of the Gang. They didn't go back to class after the interview with Mr Storey. Naomi looked quite put out, not knowing what had happened to lover boy.

'Come on,' Dad says, shoving me. 'Race you down to that gate.'

It's steep but, what the heck, he wants a race, I'll give him a race. Next moment we're skipping and bounding over the hard ground. I hit the gate first and look back. Dad's following, taking these silly, little steps on account of the gradient. The way he's running makes him look really stupid. A couple of the Green Welly and Walking Stick Brigade shake their heads.

'Dad,' I tell him. 'You run like a girl.'

'Sexist,' he chuckles.

'You can't say that to me,' I retort. 'Girls can't be sexist.'

Dad pulls a face. 'I don't see why not.'

Mum and Lauren are approaching at a more sedate pace. They've taken the long way round.

'Annie,' Dad says. 'It is all over, isn't it, this business with John?'

'Yes,' I reassure him.

That's when I feel it.

John's tug.

Annie

Sunday, 5th October

Bryony's just been on the phone. It doesn't look like Mr Storey is planning to involve the police. I didn't expect him to. I don't even know if there is much the police could do anyway, after all this time. I don't seriously think that's what I wanted. I had to have it out in the open. Now everybody will know. It's a little while after I hang up that I find myself staring at the phone. How does Bryony know the outcome of the interview? It doesn't take long for me to answer my own question. She's obviously been talking to Matthew for some time, behind my back if you like. Odd thing, that: your best friend conducting secret meetings with . . . hang on, what is Matthew to me, exactly? What's totally weird is the way that I feel a pang of jealousy, as if I think something is developing between Bryony and Matthew. Oh, behave yourself, Annie. What are you saying? Why should I care anyway? This is up to Bryony. She can make her own decisions. But not this one, I find myself murmuring, not Matthew.

'Annie?' Dad's knocking on my bedroom door.

'Yes?'

'I'm just popping out. Lauren's coming with me.'

Mum's working so I'm going to be in on my own. Not a big deal really, when you're sixteen, but that's the way families are. They sign in and sign out. Protocol.

'Where are you going?'

Dad waits a beat. 'Katie Sorrel is coming round for her tea. Your mum talked it over with Mrs Sorrel last night.'

'Oh . . . right.'

'You're OK with this, aren't you?'

I nod. 'Sure, why wouldn't I be?'

Exactly, why wouldn't I be?

Tea is odd. Dad's cooking, for starters. It's nothing special, the usual kiddie-gunk menu: freezer pizza, spaghetti hoops, microwave chips. No, the food isn't odd. It's the atmosphere round the table. Lauren and Katie keep glancing at each other, then at me, like I'm going to throw some major wobbler, which I'm not. I'm all wobbled out. See, this is me, dis-wobbled woman.

'I'm going to finish my homework,' I announce, excusing myself from the table.

I can feel three pairs of eyes following me out of the room. Jeez, make a girl feel uncomfortable, why don't you?

Ten minutes later I hear Dad clearing the tea things.

'Do you need a hand?' I ask.

Dad grins and holds out his hands. There's a dish cloth in one and a tea towel in the other.

'Wash or wipe?' he says.

'Wash. You always leave smears.'

Dad puts on a horrified face. 'I do not!'

'So why does Mum make you wash the dishes twice?'

'OK,' he says. 'You wash. I'll wipe.'

We watch the girls wandering around the back lawn, talking. We can hear their voices floating through the open window.

We're just finishing off when the phone rings.

'Do you mind putting the dishes away?' Dad says. 'I'll get that.'

'Sure,' I say. 'No problem.'

I'm stacking the plates when I hear the girls talking outside. Lauren is telling Katie about her secret place. That's the cupboard under the stairs to the rest of us. Lauren sits there sometimes when she's in a strop or when she wants to be alone with her thoughts.

'I've got a secret place,' Katie says.

Her voice drops so I can barely hear her.

'It used to be John's.'

*

It's an hour before I get my chance to ask Katie what she meant. Lauren is in the kitchen, talking to Dad, begging him to let Katie stay another hour – *just* another hour. Dad is trying to explain that it isn't up to him. Katie is in the living room, staring out of the window.

'The colours are lovely, aren't they?' she says. 'I like autumn.'

'Yes,' I say. 'Sometimes it looks like the trees are on fire.'

I hesitate then, knowing I can't hesitate too long or Lauren will be back, I go for it.

'I overheard you talking about your secret place.' Hurriedly, I add, 'I had one when I was your age.'

'Where?'

'At the bottom of the garden. It was our old shed. It's knocked down now.'

Easy does it, I tell myself. 'So where's your secret place?'

Katie cocks her head. 'If I tell you, it won't be a secret, will it?'

'Oh, go on. I won't let on.'

Katie glances round conspiratorially. 'It's the gazebo,' she whispers. 'You know what a gazebo is?'

'Yes, of course. I didn't know you had one.'

'It's behind the conifers at the bottom of the garden. Dad planted them so we'd have a quiet area for barbecues.'

I can imagine it in my mind's eye, the concealed summer house at the end of the Sorrels' garden.

'Dad built it a few years ago,' Lauren says. 'It's got a window seat and everything.' She tells me more but I don't really take it in. So that's what you meant, John. Now I understand.

Annie

Wednesday, 8th October

It wasn't the ten thousand ships that defeated Troy. It wasn't the armies of the Greeks. It wasn't even the gods. It was the wooden horse that breached the walls of the citadel. The blow came from within.

I think I already know what I'll find in the missing pages. It was there all the time. I got so obsessed with my mission, I just couldn't look beyond the Gang. I was too busy playing the avenging angel to think clearly. John told me often enough. No matter how often they hurt him, no matter how many times they humiliated him, they couldn't get to the heart of him. They couldn't make him hate himself. That would take more than they had.

'Annie,' Mrs Linklater says, looking up from her palm pilot, 'are you with us today?'

I turn my eyes towards her. 'I am,' I say.

She smiles though there is nothing reflected in her eyes. The fall-out from Matthew's confession is still reverberating around the school. Luke Woodford's parents are kicking up a stink. They refuse to admit he's done anything wrong. They're calling Matthew a liar. They're even threatening to move Luke to another school. Bryony reckons Mr Storey is hoping they're not bluffing.

'I've just called out your name three times,' Mrs Linklater explains.

Everybody is looking in my direction, everybody except Matthew that is. He is simply staring ahead. He seems to do that a lot. I think it's his way of handling the isolation. Going to Mr Storey hasn't earned him any respect from the other kids. Most of the boys are giving him the cold shoulder. They might not agree with what the Gang did to John but nobody likes a grass.

Registration over, the form spills into the corridor.

'Bryony,' I say, 'will you do me a favour?'

She gives me a sidelong glance.

'It's no big deal,' I say. 'But, if my mum or dad ask you anytime, I was with you Friday night.'

Bryony frowns. 'Last Friday?'

With a shake of the head, I correct her. 'No,' I say, 'the day after tomorrow.'

The frown stays. 'So what's happening this Friday?'

She thinks the John thing is over. I'm not going to worry her. 'I'm seeing someone.'

Bryony instinctively glances at Matthew.

'Someone else,' I tell her.

'Do tell.'

'Nothing to tell,' I say. 'I want to keep him secret.'

'From me?'

'From everybody.'

Bryony doesn't look quite convinced. Doubt lingers in her eyes. 'What's with all the mystery?' she asks.

'It's nothing,' I say. 'I don't want to go public yet. So will you cover for me?'

'OK,' Bryony says.

Grudging isn't the word for it. To be honest, I wouldn't believe me. Bryony isn't quite done. 'You wouldn't . . .?'

'What?'

Suspicion is replaced by resignation. 'Forget it,' Bryony says.

She's right not to trust me, of course. I got the idea on Sunday. Lauren and Katie are having a sleep-over this Friday night, at our house this time. Katie mentioned that her mum and dad don't mind. I'm the one they object to, not Lauren. The Sorrels are going out for a meal. It's their wedding anniversary. This is my chance. I'm going round there. I'm going to find those missing pages.

'I feel sorry for Matthew,' Bryony says as we line up outside the computer suite.

'How's that?'

'Oh, come on, Annie. You know. He did all this for you. Now you're seeing somebody else.'

Matthew is standing apart, flicking through his school planner. His eyes aren't focusing on the page. He might as well be holding it upside down.

'I didn't ask him to rat out his mates,' I say. 'That was down to you.'

'Honestly, Annie,' Bryony says. 'You can be really cold sometimes.'

I let the comment go. What more is there to say?

from John's diary
Sunday, 11th May

If you're reading this, then I counted wrong. Taking pills is like Russian roulette. There's one bullet in the chamber. That leaves five empty clicks, one big explosion. It's good odds. That's how I called it. I expected a click, then the slow walk back to life. It's simple. I get the dosage right, people finally notice. They stop the hurt. I get it wrong, what the hell, the pain is over anyway. They say an attempt on your life is a cry for help. Maybe. The way I see it, it's a wake-up call. Your son is breaking, Mum. I want the torture to end.

But you're not Mum, are you, dear reader? Mum isn't the one who has the compass to my feelings, the North, South, East and West of me. My own mother and she doesn't have a clue what makes me tick. The hands holding these pages belong to you, don't they, Annie? It's got to be you. Nobody else would bother to come looking. Nobody else cares. I'm right, aren't I? It is you, isn't it Annie? You came back. You came home. To me. Live or die, that's worth something. You cared. You were the one person in the whole stinking world who did.

I love you, Annie, but you don't love me, do you, at least not the way I want to be loved. Right through that holiday in America, I tried to tell myself different, but I'm no fool. In the end I stopped kidding myself. Don't worry, I don't think any less of you for it. I don't think any less of myself, either. The only thing I regret – I don't quite know how to say this – if I came on strong that time in the pool, I'm sorry. I wouldn't ever hurt you, Annie. You brought me back to life. You offered me friendship when nobody else gave a damn.

You're surprised I know how you felt? Like I said, I'm not daft. I tried to fool myself. I suppose I was living a fantasy. It works for a while but you can't carry on like that for long. There was no

150

disguising the little looks, the way you shrank, ever so slightly, from my touch.

This is weird, you know. Either I am writing to nobody, making silly little marks on paper that will never be read, or I've messed up and I am writing from beyond the grave. Looks like I'll never write the Great British Novel, just my own epitaph: John Sorrel, loved many, was loved by nobody.

Feel good about yourself, Annie. You did the right thing. You're the best thing that ever happened to me.

Annie
Friday, 10th October

I'm sitting on the window seat in the twilight. I'm numb. I've just read the missing pages, from the first entry where John describes the quarrel with his father to the last terrible goodbye. The stripping incident is here and a lot more besides. The things they said they were going to do! I feel sick. I half-knew what was in these pages but that didn't make them any easier to read. John should have left well alone. But, like the little boy who keeps tugging at the dog's tail, he just had to keep on at it. After that first time, when his dad let it slip in Florida, he couldn't get the words out of his head.

Your mum, he said, *you think she's such an angel. Always there for you, eh? If you only . . .*

Was there really a secret or was it just another of the Stress Hound's many instruments of emotional torture? Finally, one evening, John pushed and probed until he got his answer. I've read his account, read it twice over, from start to finish. I can see the scene as clearly as if I am watching the re-run of an old soap on TV. 'Go on then,' John yells. 'Tell me your stupid secret. You think it'll make any difference? I couldn't hate you any more than I already do. Tell me.' He keeps at it. Over and over again he says it: tell me. Go on, knock yourself out, big shot. It is an act of revenge. It makes him stronger, braver, better able to survive. Tell me your big secret. Do your worst. In the end, Mr Sorrel snaps. All these years he has been dying to say it. But when he does, it is as if someone has unpicked the seam of reality. Darkness oozes through the yawning gap. The words still rebounding off the walls, John's face drains of blood. Already Stress Hound is babbling, stammering out excuses, trying to take it back.

'John, I'm sorry. You pushed me too hard. John, you've got to forgive me.'

But John knows him too well. He understands the full extent of his self-interest. Long past believing Stress Hound has a single ounce of concern for him, John lashes out. 'All this begging, it isn't because you love me, or care how I feel. It's because you don't want Mum to know you've told me. You're scared, that's all.'

There is no forgiveness. The waves roll back leaving contempt as driftwood on the tide line. For a moment John stands staring. Then he breaks and runs, out of the house, up the road, running into traffic with barely a moment's attention for the blaring horns or squealing tyres. He is gone for hours, walking, sitting on a park bench, his heart kicked out. All those years, all the jibes, and all for something as stupid, pointless as this. He comes home late. Mum is waiting for him. He expected it. They talk. Hour after hour they talk. She tries to explain, to make sense of it. But in the end, there is no sense to be made. John is lost. The one thing he needs from her, she can't give.

Seeing the dark closing around me, I walk round to the front door. Slipping the sheaf of pages into the plastic wrapper in which I found them, I post them through the Sorrels' letter box.

'Enjoy,' I say as the flap snaps behind the package, a brutal crack of finality.

I walk home.

Annie

Saturday, 11th October

I know who it is the moment I hear the doorbell.

'I was expecting you,' I say, answering the door.

Mrs Sorrel looks past me into the hall. Her eyes flick nervously from side to side. 'Are your parents in?' she asks.

'No,' I say. 'They've gone shopping. Lauren's with them.' I lead the way into the living room. Picking up the remote, I turn off the TV. I wasn't watching it anyway.

'John's diary,' she says. 'You're the one who found it.' It's a statement, not a question. I don't even grace it with an answer.

'You must hate us,' she says.

Still no reply. I've got nothing to say.

'Don't think too badly of Phil,' she says. 'I hurt him very badly.'

'He hurt John worse,' I say.

Mrs Sorrel hangs her head. Is it shame or simply the admission that she has said the wrong thing? 'Yes.'

'What do you want, Mrs Sorrel?' I ask. 'Forgiveness? You won't get any here. You and your husband did this to John just as much as those boys who pursued him. You're worse. They were strangers. He expected nothing from them. You were meant to be there for him.'

'You're right,' she says. 'Yes, you're right. We allowed ourselves to get caught up in our own problems. We let him down.'

'Maybe you should go,' I say.

By way of reply she sits down on the settee. 'Please let me explain,' she says, twisting her wedding ring. 'I don't ask you to forgive. I don't even ask you to understand.'

She catches my eye. In the fish-cold pupils there is the spark of a plea. 'Phil and I were happy at first,' she says, starting her confessional, 'really in love. We had something special.'

I want to stop her. There's nothing she can say that will absolve her or her husband for what has happened.

'Then Jessica was born. I got the baby blues, such a stupid expression, post-natal depression they call it now. If you haven't been through it, you just can't understand.' Getting no encouragement from me, she continues. 'Suddenly I was a different person. I simply couldn't function. I fell into a dark tunnel. Annie, I thought I was going mad.'

I just look on, listening. Seeing there is still no response, Mrs Sorrel continues.

'By the time I came out of it, Phil had changed. He had grown to resent me. He couldn't understand what I'd been through. It was his turn to be cold to me. Crazy, isn't it, how things can go so badly wrong between two people who love each other? Anyway, we didn't talk. It got worse. He resented me. I resented him back. Eventually . . . ' Her voice trails off.

'You had the affair,' I say.

'Yes.'

Then she actually said it, the same corny cliché you get in every soap opera.

'It didn't mean anything. His name was Andrew Robinson, my boss at work. He gave me a shoulder to cry on. He made me feel wanted for the first time in months.'

I finish the story. 'Which is how you got pregnant with John.'

'Yes. Annie, if I could turn the clock back I would.'

'Yes,' I say, 'I know.' But there is no sympathy in my voice. I know neither she nor her husband meant any of this. People have affairs. They hurt each other. It happens. The point is, they took out their disappointments on John. He became their battleground.

Mrs Sorrel sighs. 'Phil forgave me,' she says. 'Kind of . . .'

'But he didn't forgive John.'

She shakes her head. 'I think he tried. He just couldn't feel any love for another man's son. My baby became a constant reminder of what I'd done. Phil allowed his resentment towards me to poison his feelings for John.'

'But fifteen years!' I cry, finally showing my feelings. 'How could he keep it up for fifteen years?'

It is Mrs Sorrel's turn to fall silent.

'OK,' I say, 'so maybe he was angry. But to keep it up for fifteen years, to hurt a little boy's feelings all that time . . . it's horrible. It's torture.'

'Yes,' Mrs Sorrel says.

'It's so immature, so infantile, so self-destructive . . .' For a moment I'm lost for words. 'It's as if he enjoyed playing the victim. He wanted to wallow in it. But he wasn't the victim, was he, Mrs Sorrel? John was. Your son.'

Her cold eyes flash, just for a moment. 'Phil's a good man,' Mrs Sorrel says, irritation creeping into her voice. 'He just couldn't come to terms with what happened.'

'I bet he made a big deal of taking in another man's son,' I say. 'Yes, he'd be a great martyr. I bet he never let you forget you'd made a mistake.' I'm angry with the pair of them. All I can see is John, hurt and confused, not knowing why things were never right. 'For goodness' sake, Mrs Sorrel. This isn't the old days. People forgive.'

'You won't forgive me,' she says pointedly.

I pause, then answer. 'That's right, Mrs Sorrel,' I say. 'I won't. You and your husband, you're adults. You let your problems get in the way of making your own son happy. How could you be so self-indulgent? How could you be so cruel?'

Mrs Sorrel turns to go. 'I don't think there's any more to say.'

'No?' I say, 'well I do. You were his mother. His mother, for goodness' sake. Not his guardian, not a friend, not his aunty, his *mum*!' My voice is raised but I don't care. 'You should have been there for him. Nothing's more important than that. Are you so dried-up inside you couldn't see what was going on?'

The way she stands there taking it, I want to shake her, make her fight back. Anything but this inert silence.

'What kind of woman are you?'

All there has been is a single moment of irritation.

'Annie,' she says, still calm, still resigned. 'You're young. You don't understand.'

'Don't patronise me, Mrs Sorrel,' I snap back. 'I'm old enough to know what you've done.'

I wait a beat, then finish what I was saying. 'Or what you didn't do.'

Does nothing bother this woman? Suddenly I want to hurt her. 'You let him down every day of his life,' I yell. 'You make me sick.'

Finally, she snaps. 'Do you think I don't care?' she screams, the façade shattering like a crystal. 'Is that it? Well, you're wrong, Annie. Can you even begin to imagine how I felt, reading those entries, when he knew it was you, not me, holding those pages? You were there for him and I wasn't. What does that say about me? Every day, every waking moment since John died I've hated myself. I betrayed my own child, Annie. I let him fall in despair.' At last the dam broke and she sobbed out the rest. 'If it wasn't for Katie . . .' She breaks off and fumbles for a tissue. 'If it wasn't for her,' she continues, her voice teetering on a knife-edge of pain and self-loathing, 'then I would be happy to follow John.'

I don't know how to feel any more. I'm still angry but maybe there's the faintest trace of pity. She meets my eyes. 'Since he died, every day has been a living hell for me. Judge me if you want, Annie, but please, you mustn't ever think I don't care.'

It takes her a few moments before she can compose herself. At the front door she turns round. 'Are you going to mention this to your parents?'

'No, I won't say anything.'

She looks surprised.

'I'm not doing it for you,' I explain. 'I'm trying to do something that you never did for John. I'm thinking about somebody other than myself. Lauren likes having Katie as a friend. Why should I make her unhappy over this?'

Without another word, Mrs Sorrel walks out of the door and goes to the car. Her husband is sitting in the driver's seat. For the briefest moment our eyes meet. He is the one to look away. At least he has the decency to feel ashamed. I watch the car pull away and turn the corner. Taking a deep breath I walk back indoors.

Annie

Monday, 13th October

'Swear,' I say. 'Promise you'll never breathe a word to anyone.'

'You know me better than that, Annie,' Bryony says.

I do too. These last few weeks we've changed, Bryony and me. We've grown up. I suppose we've had to. She's not the fluffy, frothy teenager she was. Until I put her to the test, I didn't know quite what a wonderful friend she was. I know I can trust her with anything.

'You're not going to let on to your parents then?' she asks.

'Never.' My thoughts flash to last night. I went over to them just before bedtime. I gave Mum a kiss then asked Dad for one of his big bear hugs. I don't know if they understood – I think they did – but it was my way of telling them it was over. I'd drawn a line in the sand.

'And you're happy for Lauren to visit that house?' Bryony asks.

'The Sorrels failed John,' I tell her. 'They're not going to do the same with Katie.'

Bryony sighs. 'I suppose not.' Her eyes are drifting across the school yard. 'What about Matthew?' she says.

The skin on my back quivers. He's just a few metres away, alone, the same as he has been every day since the bust-up with Luke.

'What about him?'

'It's the one item of unfinished business, Annie. You must know that.'

'What's unfinished about it?'

Bryony shakes her head. 'If you don't know, I can't tell you.

158

He's sorry, Annie. Surely you know that.'

I know what I think about most things, about John, about the Sorrels, about Mum and Dad. There can't be many kids my age more sure of how they feel. But Matthew? He's the one variable in all this. I mean, I know what I think. He did wrong. OK, maybe he was never the ringleader, maybe he took a step back, maybe he even did his best to put things right. But *forgive* him? How could I ever do that? There you go, that's what I think. But thinking isn't the problem. It's the way I feel that's giving me all the grief. Try as I might, I can't shut him out. I see those blue eyes, like sapphires, burning into me. And when I feel his touch, the slightest brush of his skin against mine, it's as if I've found another, better, way of being alive.

'You're going to have to talk to him, Annie.'

It's my turn to sigh. 'What do I say?'

'Oh honestly, Annie, just tell him *something*.'

Matthew is over by the railings, watching the traffic rumble by. At least, that's what he is pretending to do. All he's really doing is staying out of the way of Luke, Michael and Anthony. Not that they are likely to do anything. Their power is broken. People have finally realised they're trouble.

'Hi,' I say.

Matthew's face floods with pleasure, then the glow dies as quickly as it appeared. I expect to feel John tug at me. Nothing.

'Hi,' Matthew answers.

'Bryony says we've got to talk.'

Matthew grins. 'She's all right, Bryony.'

'Yes,' I say. 'She is.' I wait. 'You're finding this hard, aren't you?'

'Everybody thinks I'm a grass.'

'They don't think much of the other three, either,' I say.

Matthew gives a wry smile. 'That's a big comfort.'

He sees Luke, Michael and Anthony watching and walks to a corner of the yard, just out of sight.

'You did the right thing,' I say, following him. I'm suddenly aware that we are alone, behind the kitchen. If the lunchtime supervisors spot us, we'll get a detention.

'But?'

'How did you know there's a but?'

Matthew frowns. 'There's always a but.'

'Look,' I say, 'I know you think I'm hard. Matthew, I just can't forget what you did. There can be no you and me.'

'I've tried to put it right,' he says.

'I know and I respect you for that. But to feel something for you, I've got to be sure there isn't even a shred of cruelty in you. How can I, with everything I know?'

There's no disguising the fractured expression in Matthew's eyes. 'Everybody makes mistakes, Annie. We go along with things we shouldn't. Somebody's being hurt, most people turn a blind eye. Don't tell me you haven't done that.'

I shrug.

'Nobody's perfect,' he says. 'Nobody gets it right all the time. But we change. I've done that.'

'Matthew, you're probably right. It's just . . . I can't forget.'

That's when his hands reach out. I feel the pressure of his fingers on my upper arms. He draws me close and presses his lips to mine. Still I expect John to tug at me, remind me who Matthew is, what he did. I want to pull away but the touch of his lips, his breath, they ease away all the hurt. I want this feeling to go on forever. I want to let myself dissolve and be part of him. Then the bell rings, announcing the end of the lunch hour. I put my hands on Matthew's chest and push him away. I grimace. This is something I've done before.

'I've got to go.'

'But you'll see me again? Annie, please? I've lost all my friends. My parents are ashamed of me. I've got nothing any more. Tell me at least you care.'

'I can't do it.'

I jog away, my neck hot, the brush of his lips still on mine. Still no tug from John.

'Annie,' Matthew calls after me. 'If you mean it, if there can be no us, turn that corner and don't look back.'

This I can do. I know it. I've done harder things. I got justice for John. Straightening my hair, I start to turn the corner. Then,

160

just for a fleeting moment, my eyes meet Matthew's. As I reach Bryony waiting by the science block I can still see the ghost of his smile.

Bullying! You can stop it!
Over 20,000 young people get help every year when they speak out against bullying.
One Life available 24/7 at www.bbc.co.uk/radio1/onelife

Blood Pressure

For the boy who has everything – here's a little something extra:

- Swap the happy family home in leafy suburbia for a dodgy Northern estate, home of your dying grandfather.
- Swap the gorgeous Emily for Jade. She's got a few secrets of her own. You don't want to know. Really.
- Swap those loving parents for turf wars, crime, drugs and a stranger who, incredibly, claims to be your father.

This isn't one of those dreams you wake up from – for fifteen-year-old Aidan it's a slice of life that is all too real.

A sensational thriller that will raise your blood pressure and set your pulse racing.

The Edge

Danny is a boy on the edge. A boy teetering on the brink of no return, living in fear.

Cathy is his mother. She's been broken by fear.

Chris Kane is fear – and they belong to him.

But one day they escape. They're looking for freedom, for the promised land where they can start really living. Instead they find prejudice, and danger of another kind.

Uncompromising and disturbing, but utterly readable, this Alan Gibbons novel positively crackles with tension as he writes about a mother and her son desperate to start a new life.

Shortlisted for the Carnegie Medal.

Caught in the Crossfire

'You know what happens to people like you? You get hit in the crossfire.'

Shockwaves sweep the world in the aftermath of 11 September. The Patriotic League barely need an excuse in their fight to get Britain back for the British, but this is chillingly perfect.

Rabia and Tahir are British Muslims, Daz and Jason are out looking for trouble, Mike and Liam are brothers on different sides. None of them will escape unscarred from the terrifying and tragic events which will weave their lives together.

Marking a new dimension in his writing on race, riots and real life, *Caught in the Crossfire* is an unforgettable novel that Alan Gibbons needed to write.

'Gibbons' writing often addresses worrying issues of social justice but never as powerfully as in this novel . . . the writing – short, sharp pieces that take us into the mind of each character – is accessible and compulsive.'

Wendy Cooling, *The Bookseller*

The Dark Beneath

'Today I shot the girl I love.'

GCSEs are over and sixteen-year-old Imogen is looking forward to a perfect, lazy English summer. But her world is turned upside down by three refugees, all hiding from life. Anthony is fourteen, already an outcast, bullied and shunned by his peers. Farid is an asylum seeker from Afghanistan, who has travelled across continents seeking peace. And Gordon Craig is a bitter, lonely man. She knows all of them, but she doesn't know how dangerous they are. Being part of their lives could cost Imogen her own.

Supercharged with tension and drama, Alan Gibbons' novel is about what happens when the fabric of normality is ripped apart, exposing the terrifying dark beneath.

The Defender

When Kenny Kincaid turns his back on the past he has no idea of the legacy he is bequeathing his only son, Ian.

Was he escaping from the paramilitaries, from too much violence and bloodshed, too many victims? Or was he betraying the Cause, turning his back on his comrades-in-arms when he fled clutching his baby son and quarter of a million pounds from a bank job? They think so, and they're intent on revenge. Years later Kenny is still a target – and now so is Ian.

Father and son are going to have to live with it . . . or die with it.

Controversial and compulsive reading, this is an unputdownable thriller.

'Alan Gibbons can always be relied upon to raise pulse rates, and his *The Defender* is . . . achingly exciting'

Independent

The Lost Boys' Appreciation Society

Something was wrong. The anger-flash had drained out of Dad's face, replaced by a blank pallor. Like disbelief . . .

When Mum was killed in a car crash our lives were wrecked too.

Gary, John and Dad are lost without Mum. Gary is only 14 and goes seriously off the rails, teetering on the brink of being on the wrong side of the law. John is wrestling with GCSEs and his first romance – but he's carrying the burden of trying to cope with Gary and Dad at the same time. And they're all living with the memories of someone they can never replace.

Alan Gibbons writes with compassion – and flashes of humour – about surviving against all the odds.

Shadow of the Minotaur

'Real life' or the death defying adventures of the Greek myths, with their heroes and monsters, daring deeds and narrow escapes – which would you choose?

For Phoenix it's easy. He hates his new home and the new school where he is bullied. He's embarrassed by his computer geek dad. But when he logs on to The Legendeer, the game his dad is working on, he can be a hero. He is Theseus fighting the terrifying Minotaur, or Perseus battling with snake-haired Medusa.

The trouble is The Legendeer is more than just a game. Play it if you dare.

Vampyr Legion

What if there are real worlds where our nightmares live and wait for us?

Phoenix has found one and it's alive. Armies of blood-sucking vampyrs and terrifying werewolves, the creatures of our darkest dreams, are poised to invade our world.

But Phoenix has encountered the creator of *Vampyr Legion*, the evil Gamesmaster, before and knows that this deadly computer game is for real – he must win or never come back.

Warriors of the Raven

The game opens up the gateway between our world and the world of the myths.

The Gamesmaster almost has our world at his mercy. Twice before fourteen-year-old Phoenix has battled against him, in *Shadow of the Minotaur* and *Vampyr Legion*, but Warriors of the Raven is the game at its most complex and deadly level. This time, Phoenix enters the arena for the final conflict, set in the world of Norse myth. Join Phoenix in Asgard to fight Loki, the Mischief-maker, the terrifying Valkyries, dragons and fire demons – and hope for victory. Our future depends on him.

Julie and Me . . . and Michael Owen Makes Three

It's been a year of own goals for Terry.

— Man U, the entire focus of his life (what else is there?)
  lose to arch-enemies Liverpool FC
— he looks like Chris Evans, no pecs
— Mum and Dad split up (just another statistic)
— he falls seriously in love with drop dead gorgeous Julie.
  It's bad enough watching Frisky Fitzy (school golden boy)
  drool all over her, but worse still she's an ardent Liverpool FC supporter.

Life as Terry knows it is about to change in this hilariously
funny, sometimes sad, utterly readable modern Romeo and
Juliet story.

Julie and Me: Treble Trouble

For one disastrous year Terry has watched Julie, the girl of his dreams, go out with arch-rival Frisky Fitz, seen his mum and dad's marriage crumble and his beloved Man U go the same way. 2001 has got to be better.

— Will he get to run his hands through the lovely Julie's raven tresses?
— What happens when his new streamlined mum gets a life?
— Can Man U redeem themselves and do the business in the face of the impossible?

Returning the love – that's what it's all about.

Read the concluding part of *Julie and Me* and all will be revealed.